Creative Writing Heals
Volume 2

A new collection from Converge writers
at York St John University 2019

Creative Writing Heals: Volume 2
First published in 2019
by Writing Tree Press

The moral rights of the authors have been asserted.
All characters and events in this publication, other than those clearly in the public domain, are fictitious, and any resemblance to any real person, living or dead, is purely coincidental and not intended by the authors.

The right of Helen Kenwright to be identified as the editor of this work has been asserted by her in accordance with Section 77 of the Copyright, Designs and Patents Act 1988

For information contact:
Writing Tree Press, Unit 10773, PO Box 4336
Manchester, M61 0BW
www.writingtree.co.uk

Dedication

For everyone who finds words to be a light in the darkness, a comfort in the cold and a door to better days.

Contents

Caroline SB

v

vi

x

Foreword

A year ago we put together the first 'Creative Writing Heals' as a way of celebrating our students' writing and giving them a voice. It happened with all the rush and excitement of a new idea with a challenging deadline, borne of adrenaline and a stubborn denial of the impossible.

This year we've had more time to plan and prepare for our second volume, inspired and enthused by the success of the first. We hoped that by giving students more time they'd be able to produce work they could feel proud of. As so often, I underestimated them. Our students didn't just produce good work. They worked week after week with their mentors to polish and improve their pieces. Many found themselves facing for the first time all the fears and barriers of submitting work for publication, of putting their work out there for others to read and respond to. One student told me, 'It's like the difficult second album. We have something to live up to now. A reputation we don't want to ruin'.

Through the hard work and dedication of students and mentors alike, our Converge Creative Writing students have produced work which exceeded my expectations. The whole team is proud of what they have achieved. So kick off your shoes, curl up in your favourite spot, relax and enjoy this lavish buffet from Converge creative writers!

Helen Kenwright

May, 2019

The Test of Life
Sandra Phillips

It is a constant repetitive cycle between life and death
wanting to live, whilst fearing dying
the Groundhog Day becoming overwhelming
the negative storyline becoming soul-destroying
living in a world where there is no
Beginning
Middle
End.
just the same repeated thoughts going through
everybody's mind
trying to change the damaging repetition
to positive affirmations
it is a constant repetitive cycle between life and
death.

To achieve is to succeed.
when there is something to aspire to
a positive outcome, a particular thought, or process
to succeed is to gain control
to learn coping mechanisms to change
Negative
To
Positive.
engaging in education enables a positive sense of self
aiming for a desired result
pursuing as many aspects of life as possible
meaning, purpose and happiness
to achieve is to succeed.

What It Means to Me
Junior Mark Cryle

Determined to see that a task reach its conclusion,
willing to put grudges aside to achieve a goal.

Reliable in times of urgency and importance,
truly an ally you can depend on.

Adapts to make a problem work for you,
to find a way forward when none can be found.

Greed drives you to keep what you hold dear,
for the happiness they bring and the memory they
contain.

Optimism provides incentive to move forward,
proof that life is not as bleak as it seems.

Nostalgia may often keep you from accepting
change,
but to prepare for the future one must learn from the
past.

Words are defined by the meaning we give them.
These are but examples of what I see when I think of:
DRAGON.

Collected Poems
Holly

Catching Stars

Dragging them closer
      close enough to touch
      close enough to burn his hands
      close enough to burn his skin.
It was nicer to imagine
      he thought
than to tear pieces from the night sky.
            The planets were no longer aligned
      in their comforting embrace.
The moon glared down
      disorientated.
He felt choked by the suffocating darkness.
      Like jigsaw pieces
he would have to reunite them.

Fortress

We used to build kingdoms, their foundations stood on puddles. Now we glance out, observing rain drops in single file, weakening defences like toy knights waging a relentless war against the window panes, eventually seeping through like memories of our imagination we were once unable to contain. We were warriors against the weather, now we hide under umbrella defences.

Spring benches

Life returns
regenerates
revives
as the leaves turn green once more.
Lives which have ended
memorized on plaques.
Providing a soothing place to observe
what they had once admired.

A Dystopian Triptych
Joanne Platt

Part 1
Swimming Lessons for Baby Frogs

I'm on a lilo bobbing on the water. I part the waves, slip under the surface. I can hold my breath for one, two …

***

It's all novel in the beginning. Our world turned topsy turvy. Ducks waddle in as anyone who can ships out. We wade around a diorama of random objects caught up and agitated in the whorls of whipped chocolate water that yesterday was our town.

As the water level rises we rub bulging eyes with stubby fingers to bring this new world into focus. A rubbish dump Venice. Murk-brown. Our homes half under water, half in air.

A child's doll comes careering round the corner carried on the current. Its eyes thick lashed; its plastic lids unnaturally open, unblinking; its glassy eyeballs turned up to the sun. Its hard little body beats rhythmically against the brickwork of the corner terrace we'd kicked our football against monotonously through languid summer evenings.

It's then I see them, mistaking them at first for shop dummies. Grotesque versions of the doll these bodies float face down, outstretched. As if they'd headed out for an early morning constitutional and stopped instead to drink in the cocoa brown liquid.

The barn on the hilltop is now a makeshift morgue. When the bodies are too many, men in yellow hazmats sink them to the riverbed with rocks.

The Floods, or The Swellings as we come to call them, are our new moon-tides.

Families set sail like the Owl and the Pussycat on children's paddling pools.
    We narrow our nostrils against the stench of death.
    And desperation.
    Wait for help to come down from The Drylands.

When I see my reflection in the ripples, I see my body changing as sure as the world around me is changing.

The floating carcasses like giant otherworldly jellyfish with their bloated heads and garments fanning out around them, prompt my father to give me my first lesson in Underwater Survival. He shows me how to pinch my nostrils together with my finger stumps. How to bend my legs and let my body fall supported by the water until my head dips below the surface. How to count while I hold my breath.
    At first my reflexes thrust me back up struggling to the surface, but soon I yield to the inrush of water to my nostrils and mouth. I come to revel in the feeling of being held by the water in a kind of sinewy web, a primordial suspension.

As my water-body becomes more natural to me than my land-body I shift my feet one in front of the other exploring the dark underbelly; the underwater factories of life and of death. My skin is livid, strangely porous. My lungs atrophied, blocked; shallow like party balloons knotted, stomachs stapled. I don't breathe; I absorb. The water is my element now.

I long for The Swellings so I can glide eel-like through the submerged windows. I smash out the frames for easy egress.

In the water I forget about my body and the way it's changing. The smells don't bother me any more. My nostrils have closed, my nose flattened to a scaly ridge. I no longer fear the changes. They've freed me to be who I am.

Secrets come sweeping out from under rocks. Things thought gone for ever are washing into plain sight.

I wonder at how fluid everything actually is. How nothing really goes away. How often we return to the place of our origins. Short-sighted, the big picture lies often in our blind spots and it takes more than a change of perspective to see things go in cycles not lines. Why shouldn't we go backwards as well as forwards? And maybe there's no such thing anyway because it all depends where you draw the line in the sand in the first place - or the riverbed in this case.

The waters were our very first hatching grounds.

I think we were always meant to go back to the ocean.

"Two thirds of the world's surface is covered with water and yet we call it Earth. Such is man's arrogance."[1]

What would someone from The Drylands say if they could see us now?

Amphibian! Our necks all but disappeared. Our heads pointed upwards. Our eyes lidless and bulging. Our skin scaly. Our noses non-existent; mouths thin slits.

They didn't see us.

They never came.

They left us there. Left our little bit of land to sink into the sea.

Left us bobbing around on paddling pools and lilos garishly emblazoned with golden billed toucans and rainforest scenes.

The stuff of old myth …

Vivid lime palm leaves, purple dolphins and citrus orange octopi…

They left us stranded there under a sagging sun in that earth-brown primordial stew of the living and the dead.

Children swept out to sea sacrificed to season the deadly mix in that charnel house Atlantis.

---

[1] Mark Burgess (The Chameleons)

Who knows what goes on aboard the makeshift rafts? Who knows if those creatures, for they are now creatures, veer between faith in a god, faith in their government and a deep atavistic cannibalistic desire towards their fellow travellers?

For a moment a silver drone hovers like a mechanical dragonfly on the rising horizon just as dusk is falling. For a moment we think our prayers have been answered, but it shimmers away as quickly as it came. So quickly that we wonder if we hadn't hallucinated it after all. A flash of light in the sky. The flash of a camera? Intermittent bursts of blue-white light, a star-like symphony in the flash-lit firmament. As the scene of our sinking relays out in real time to a million screens up on The Drylands, what's left of our town slides silently to the seabed.

"And if you refuse … them … I will smite your whole territory with frogs … which will come up and go into your house and into your bedroom and on your bed, … and into your ovens and into your kneading bowls. So the frogs will come up on you …"
- Exodus 8:1-15

And so it was that where their gods and their fellow men failed them their nature did not fail them.

And being that they were not equipped for the air, but were now for the waters, they slipped in like so many eels emptied from a tin pail. Strings of slithering life-form cast back to the primeval riverbeds from which they once sprung long before they ever stepped out - visitors on a strange new land of clay and dust, of Earth that they then named as such.

And after the Great Swellings they came there again. Frogs with bulbous bodies: eyes wide and unblinking like the first men on a new planet.

I'm on a lilo bobbing on the water. I part the waves, slip under the surface ....

Part 2
Home Soil
A Week in the News

Day 0
They're no nearer to reaching an agreement. Bin bags pile up in the street like beached whales – bulbous, tightly knotted. I wonder what would happen if they were to spill out their entrails.

Day 1
For now they keep their secrets but still I close my curtains with a sense of unease

Day 2
More bags have hatched out in their nursery overnight – their bodies shiny and new. The houses around protest their innocence; proper in the dawn that

smudges the sky with its corals as it breaks.

Day 3
There's talk of bringing in a Task Force if the strike's not resolved soon. I imagine khaki camouflaged bodies grappling with the wrinkly plumpnesses. Wrestling inside the black plastic folds.

Day 4
There's been an overnight avalanche. Police are seeking the culprits in the East. Updates follow throughout the day. No one's sat glued to their television like this since the twin towers went down.

Day 5
Conspiracy theories creep out like half recognised faces from cracks in the walls. And some of those images call out to you from the back of your mind and you slam a door deep in there somewhere to stop them telling you what you already know. Only they won't stop telling you and you know that already too.

Day 6
Two people have drowned in the rubbish. These are the first deaths to have taken place on home soil and you wonder how all this is going to end.
"Chickens come home to roost," your grandfather used to say, but his time came before all this.
"In those days you knew your enemy even if you never saw his face. There wasn't that belief then that drove," he said.

In a bedsit in Camberwell a boy's strapping himself into a weighted jacket. But this jacket's not for life it's for death he thinks and to him the two become the same and he can no longer tell them apart.

"Here now is my chance," he says out loud to the camera in the corner of the room.

Day 7
The black bags out in the street rise above the level of my outside sill today. I sit on the sofa watching TV but I feel like I'm on an island floating on so much rubble and all I can see is the rising piles of flotsam outside.
If they don't come soon the streets are going to be full of rats – desert rats running around the annihilated spaces and then who's going to keep writing in this journal?

Part 3
Contact

I never doubted why they chose me to guide our guests. My reputation for guile was no secret among the higher echelons. Without having it spelt out in so many words I knew exactly what was required of me.

Our esteemed visitors did not make my task difficult. They appeared strangely uncorrupted by the carefully disguised drives that propel my own species. I wondered how much they had picked up on of our desperation. I suspected little. Having carefully stewarded the resources on their own planet they judged us by their own standards, seemingly oblivious to the manifold of darker desires that touch our kind.

They expressed surprise that the edible offerings we laid out for them were farmed not laboratory grown.

"How can you stand the blood?"

As though they believed the whole enterprise

necessitated bands of cutthroat marauding murderers wielding knives drawn sharp off some stone age flint!

I gestured to the buildings that huddle on our hillsides.

"See for yourselves?"

As we pulled up on the shit spattered cobbles the abattoir van pulled out.

"Most of it's automated these days," I told them. "The blood's only visible when the system malfunctions."

They shivered when they understood my implication catching a whiff of what must go on inside.

"Can't get rid of the smell of fear though," muttered Nickl, wrinkling his nose. I shot him a glance and he lowered his eyes.

One of their party stood out to me from the start. There was something in him I recognised. He retained some trace of the human his kindred had evolved beyond.

Ah, so some vestige remains! Our evils can't be bred out of us so easily after all.

I was strangely reassured by this. I knew his thoughts. We were brothers under the skin.

I watched his eyes glint in time to the calculations I knew were running through his mind like some rogue computer programme. That rogue remnant of the human in him had seized immediately on the advantages of our farming out – Outsourcing as we called it. It had taken the great minds of the last three centuries on earth to figure out how to cream off the fat of the land, the richest cuts whilst farming out the unwanted by-products, the unforeseen events, to regions distant and therefore far from thought. Who cares what we do in those unseen regions? That part of the enterprise can take care of itself! And so we turn a blind eye to the strange monsters that begin to grow in them.

This alien kinsman had no allegiance to anyone but himself. Well I of all men should understand that! A glint as of recognition passed between us. I resolved to speak further with him when the opportunity presented itself and present itself it did that evening at the Trade Reception.

In the flame of a candle I saw myself reflected in his lidless eye and when I excused myself from the table under some pretence it wasn't long before he followed me outside as I knew he must. The moon dangled from the firmament like a giant disco ball. It didn't take much to talk him into betraying his planet. There was too much of the human left in him after all. Ruthless greed was in his muscle memory. By the time we returned separately to the table he'd already agreed to sell out his planet's resources and I'd hatched a plan to redirect the profits from our planetary coffers depositing them into my own accounts: distributed and untraceable over the boundaries of several third world countries.

Not long after, people began to comment on the changing landscape. Buildings were appearing like fungi over the countryside in blocks shaped like letters. There were Hs and Ls, even some Os that sprung panopticon like among the more angular forms. All windowless. All having only one entrance as though what went in never came out, like the non-discharges on a hospital data sheet.

My 'friend', my partner in crime soon emerged as their leader.
Their contact with us had changed them. Their

thinking was shifting more in line with ours.

"We have learned much from you."

They bowed still but their eyes were narrower, more guarded. They eyed us intently now, nodding gently to themselves as though some seed of understanding were stirring within them.

Meanwhile out on the hillsides T blocks joined the Hs and the Ls and some among us wondered at what strange message they might comprise.

"It is time for us to return your hospitality," 'He' said eventually.

I wondered what would be in it for me.

A date was set. There was to be a banquet but beyond that we knew little, except that our guests had been won over to factory farming.

We took bets as to what might be on the menu. We fully expected our grateful visitors to offer up the best of what they had and looked forward to filling our faces at their expense.

By now I had extracted the desired knowledge of what resources their planet had that we could mine and I was officially tasked to use the evening to set up terms by which we could avail ourselves of those resources.

At six twenty I donned white dress shirt with starched collar, dinner jacket and bow tie. An Arctic penguin setting out into the frost filled evening, a myriad of stars dancing across my field of vision. Plumped up from all the diplomatic fine dining with which I'd wooed our visitors, I waddled down the street. My feet felt not a part of me and I wasn't sure that was entirely down to the bitter chill of the night air.

The banquet was to be held in the largest of the H shaped buildings. I pressed the buzzer and when the shutter lifted I entered, keen to see at last exactly what our visitors had learned from us.

Inside was even more chill than outside. My limbs stiff as if in a living rigor mortis. Stainless steel doors lined the corridor. There was a crank then a whir as of some giant thermostat clicking into action.

My frozen limbs squeezed into my pointed evening shoes, I began to glide. Relieved of the effort of lifting one foot in front of the other I was on a conveyor belt. Pirouetted around a crowded ballroom on a circular track: an automated ballerina playing to the crowd. A sea of faces bow tied, applauding me. My limbs grew ever colder. Ladies in ball gowns fanned themselves with Japanese paper fans, peering at me through opera glasses with delighted expectancy.

Gradually the excitement began to die down and a hush descended. The novelty of my entrance had worn off now. The smiling faces that surrounded me suddenly seemed to me like masks concealing all kinds of grotesqueries. Were they closing in on me or was it my imagination? The cold was an exquisite pain now, slicing into my flesh like the most delicate of filleting knives.

"Fit only for the most exquisite cuts," a visitor exclaimed leaning to sniff delicately at me and raising to his napkin a silver knife. He wiped it then set it down on his side plate, staring at me in anticipation. I looked in the direction to which all faces were turning. At the end of the conveyor belt a guillotine hung suspended over the track. I looked at my feet. They were as useless as flippers now, weighted down in a block of ice. I looked at the guillotine then I looked at my brothers and readied myself as the conveyor belt mechanism lurched suddenly forward from its standstill and hurtled towards the end.

A Light on the Shore
Llykaell Dert-Ethrae

A lone man tussles upon a boat. He is drenched in the rains that have been hammering the oak planks beneath his sodden feet and the darkening shoreline for the past hour. His net is empty. The sails strain against their pulleys, buffeted by merciless gales. The man wipes his brow of spray and deluge alike as he struggles to maintain in charge of the possessed canvas. A heavy boot squelches as it slams into the mast and the determined groan of the sailor as he grapples with the ropes in his pulsing arms is lost to the cracks of lightning and the deepest rumbles of thunder that split the ever blackening sky in twain. He cannot seem to make the distance. Just over the nearest roiling crests protrude teeth of stone so tall they seem to have belonged to the Giants of yore, yet through the lashing downpour he finds it hard to judge the gap betwixt his vessel and the ravenous maw before him. He quickly leaps, ropes in hand, to the other side of the boat, yanking with every ounce of vigour his muscles can spend. The spot is near. Only a little farther. The unruly sails need only be coaxed for a moment longer. His hand once more wipes away the torrent only to look on with widening eyes at the wave careening from his left. It crashes into him and his already soaked feet slip upon the slick beams. The hemp line is stained crimson as it passes through his tightly clenched palms. At a cost it steadies him. The man's whole body, pale and clammy, shivers but not with the cold this unforgiving nature has chosen to bestow upon him. Adrenaline courses through his veins and a steel gaze pierces from his eyes. The jaws of the rocks loom overhead. He has arrived.

Stowing the sail amidst the chaos, he moves on to haul his net over the side. It has not seen a fish in days. Neither has his stomach. Where rumours abound to feed hope to the desperate, danger is risked. Whole schools of shining scales had been spotted flocking in this locale, but only ever at dusk. Rumour or truth, it did not matter. He needed to eat.

The fruits of his despondent gamble pay him in full, though invariably at his expense. Another wall of black water rushes from the side. In a mad bid to free himself from his fate, the man yanks hard to retrieve his net, yet it catches upon one of the ravenous stones in the swirling depths. Cursing through tears at the inevitable surge hurtling toward him, the man vainly shields himself with his arms as the flood envelops his vessel and sends it soaring into the teeth. It cracks, splinters and shatters. The man is hurled like a doll into the nearest monolith and with a grotesque crunch his skull collides with it. Whilst unable to distinguish his own stars from the ones between the clouds above, his head in excruciating agony, he yields to the forces set upon destroying him and slips into darkness.

His eyes reopen to the cacophonous heavens commanding him to wake with cannonade blares resounding over the sea. Startled, he sputters and flails in the inky brine. His body is the plaything of the unrelenting waves that madly undulate as far as his salt-sprayed eyes can see. Where the shore is he cannot tell. His heart pounds so loud he hears it above the reverberating screams of the sky. Tremendous bolts of white light tear the air, illuminating the fear upon his paling features. It is only now, as the endless waters rage about that he remembers his body is near frozen and beneath the enveloping chill he shivers. Chattering teeth tremble his skull as he chooses a direction to stroke out towards, for any way is better than staying put waiting to drown. Yet nature is a cruel mistress. Chaotic currents and blinding surges of froth hinder his every effort. The man's strained efforts to defy the sadistic swells are all but in vain, for it seems the depths yearn to drag him under. The strength in his muscles is sapped by the frigid waters that constantly attempt to swallow him whole. Here, held fast in stormy jaws he struggles with ever waning efforts and as the last of his energy flows into the surrounding furore, his gaping mouth sucks in a last sweet shot of air before he is pulled beneath by the gluttonous waves.

'Twas a gamble made with such high stakes that only fools or the forlorn partake.

And yet…

His hazy eyes, staring despairingly into the crushing chilling abyss, catch sight of a dim white glow from out of the midnight depths. It slowly ascends. Bubbles spewing out from his mouth and nose to fly to the violent crests above mimic his desire to flee the nearing light. It grows brighter. Movement stirs in the deep. The man hopes he is delirious from the cold as his weakened attempts to surface do little to avoid the approach. Yet out of the blackest of blacks it arises, becoming ever clearer in his frantic eyes, but bringing with it an inexplicable swaddling of stillness within him. His brow furrows in befuddlement and his assuaged heart ceases its dramatic rhythm. Entire auroras of colour refract and dance throughout the current, captivating his darkening vision and instilling his soul with a welling serenity. His eyes shut just as the light piercing his haze splits into two prismatic lanterns of shimmering brilliance.

A blast of warmth slams into his face, rousing him. He coughs out icy brine and gulps in precious air. His limbs are frozen and cannot move yet even through their apparent numbness, defying all known reason, he feels he is laid upon air and floating over the savage rush that had failed to consume him. It crashes and swirls in a jealous rage underneath, but falls upon deaf ears for his attention, dazed though it is, centres upon the tepid air caressing his shivering skin. Gales blow over him, blasting him with a blanket of relief from the cold waters he has soared out from. The man's eyes open and close, drifting in and out of consciousness as he flies through the air on invisible wings. His journey over the sea comes to an end as he is lowered gently to the sands by this unseen force. The soft bed of granules beneath stirs him from his daze and he manages to twitch his arms and legs for the first time. He cannot sit up. He groans from the shooting agony in his skull and his vision is clouded with his own blood. The heavy raindrops allay his pain. He tries to lift his head from the ground, though barely achieves an inch, his breath catching in his throat as he does so, for an incredible sight, such as he has never beheld, unfolds before his heavy, widening eyes.

Out from the sea, a head draped in liquid gold ascends. It is followed by unearthly twin orbs of light set into a face that the gloom holds all but anonymous. A pale set of elegant shoulders rises, holding up a long white dress that sticks wetly to the graceful and slender figure gliding out from the lashing waves up towards the transfixed man. A tall woman, resolute and calm amidst the clamour in the heavens, stands silhouetted by the lightning searing the sky. It outlines her in brilliant flashes of white that glint off her soaked willowy frame. Flowing water spills from the woman's golden hair, down her long bare arms and off her majestic thin fingers in a multi-coloured cascade as it catches and reflects the shimmering gleam from her eyes. It patters to the ground and dashes against her bare feet. The hairs upon his arms raise though not out of fear, but from an unknowable energy emanating from her. There, still and silent, she regards the man with her prismatic glance. It is as if the man has drowned once more for he is unable to breathe. His limbs cry to move, yet remain stiffened. Amidst the intensity of her presence, a feeling, an aura of tranquillity, exudes from her. The man's muscles relax and he stares back at her with uncertainty and wonder, assuming he must be dead or this to be a dream. His head collapses back to the sand. She flows effortlessly around to his side in a motion so smooth it is if her feet never leave the ground. The man cannot even feel her impact the sand around him and, as curious an occurrence as that is, through the momentary illumination of another bolt from above his gawking attention is arrested instead by her face.

A fairer complexion and countenance he has never seen, yet it is hardened by experience and an insight so unfathomable he fails to repress a gasp. Her cold, yet alluring eyes stare out as expressionless as the rest of her features and beguile the man's sights. Their ever-changing and hypnotically shifting hues glint like the stars that shine between the storm clouds. All the calamity that befell him washes away as he drowns within her inscrutable gaze. He does not notice he is sat up by another invisible compulsion. Her examining stare moves from his enraptured one to the open wound upon his head and she spits into her brine soaked hand. Like a salve, she spreads it all over the gash. The threads of flesh stitch themselves back up and the bleeding stops all to the man's uncontainable amazement. Silently, she walks behind him up the beach.

Once again, the man floats up into the air and is carried through the sobering torrent. He opens his mouth to speak but there exists nothing for him to even imagine saying, yet, still curious, he tries to turn his clearing head but finds the task all too difficult. Soaring softly backward up the shore towards the cliffs and away from the monstrous waves, he sighs and feels the need to sleep once more come over him. He shakes it off. He must see his rescuer.

The man, still shivering, is placed under a slight arch just out of reach of the rain. The elegant creature stands to his left. She is staring out to sea. His mouth opens in an attempt to entreat her to conversation, yet his endeavour bears no fruit for no words issue forth. In the quiet he simply observes the fair haired beauty, yet whether or not she notices is unknown and in any event she fails to reciprocate. At long last, accompanied by another gargantuan flash from the heavens, the man's gaze is caught by movement out at sea. As was his wont around this singular woman, his uncontainable astonishment plasters his features at the sight of his wreck flying in its respective fragments towards the shore. They cease but a few feet away from the pair, the planks arranging themselves to stand upright against one another in the sand. All the while, the woman had made not a single move, yet now she steps towards the wood pile, soundless and graceful. The man watches on in startled awe as her left hand becomes engulfed in roaring flames of pitch, nigh visually indiscernible from their nocturnal surroundings but vividly distinct from the damp cold air about them for the heat from the fire coiling about her wrist and sprouting from her palm is unlike any he has previously experienced. Slowly, she extends her willowy arm toward the pyre. Such an unnatural blaze to catch along sodden timbers would be enough to astound anyone, and the man is no exception. Obsidian dances and roars along the grains of wood, consuming all. A tremendous blast of heat banishes the brisk humid air and the man sighs in relief as his skin shivers out the last remnants of chill. She turns to face him, though whatever expression is upon her face is veiled by the dark. Only her eyes light up the makeshift camp, sending calm cascading waves of light over the sands and rocks. Fighting breathlessness, he flexes his jaw and again attempts to speak to the lady, to profusely express his gratitude, but is once more muted by another inexplicable wonder manifesting before his very eyes. Rainwater, illuminated by the woman's aurora portals, dashes and splashes against an unseen surface. It collects, somehow, in the air and with no container, yet forms a semi-circle as if it is held in a bowl made of glass so clear it would be all but invisible. He only now realises how thirsty being near-drowned in the ocean has made him. The floating chromatic waters move toward him. A look of uncertainty crosses his face as he reaches out to grasp the unseen bowl. He looks to the woman. She does not move. His parched mouth yearning for its contents, his fingers avidly reach out and take hold of the container. It is like glass, smooth and cool in his palms. He wastes no time and brings it to his waiting lips, flooding his arid throat with overwhelming relief to quench, at least in part, his salt-driven thirst. Taking in a series of soothed breaths, his sight is caught by a change on the woman's face. Obscured by the black of night it is all but impossible to detect, and may be naught but a twist of the imagination - a soft rise of a smile seemingly flashes across her hidden features. The man blinks, doubting his own eyes and surely, as fast as the gesture of warmth had appeared to come, it vanishes. The woman's head turns slightly to her right, to glance sideways at the pyre. He obediently follows her line of sight to witness a stake propped against the burning wood, roasting a speared fish along its shaft. The man laughs delightedly and, shaking his head in grateful incredulity, turns back to face her.

She is gone.

Bewildered, the man calls out. Hearing no response, he painfully stands and hobbles from the small overhang to scan the beach, the horizon and the cliff face. There is nothing there but rain and wind and the clamour of the unruly sea in the distance. The man cannot stop shaking his head, but a smile does appear on his features and he shouts out his thanks to the night in the hope she will hear him.

Mirthful over his miracle, and swearing on all he holds dear never again to risk such a foolhardy undertaking, he limps back over to the fire and sits down to finish cooking his much needed meal. His smile does not last long though and as it fades from his falling face he looks wistfully out to sea. He knows who she is. They all do. She was all too poignant in the folklore of his people, yet so few had ever been granted the enviable gift of seeing her in person. The man snorts and shakes his head. Such unlikely happenstance to befall him at his most desperate hour, to be literally saved from the maw of the ocean by *her* – it is beyond the credulous limits of his friends and family and as such a bittersweet smile crawls onto his face. Yet, as he tucks ravenously into his eagerly awaited meal, he defiantly winks and gestures discourteously at the waters that had attempted so desperately to swallow him, content in the knowledge that at least he will make it home and not be food for the sea instead.

Alien Family Values
Julie Woods

Fred was fed up. No milk. How was he supposed to have breakfast for the next two weeks? He suspected that Joanne had poured it away in spite. She knew how he loved his Chocolate Aliens in slightly warmed milk. He always had done; the milk tasted of chocolate and the Aliens were squishy. He could suck off their arms and legs. It had been his favourite breakfast for at least thirty-five years.

Joanne was fed up. How could Fred have extended their stay here for another two months? Two months! They'd already been here one hundred and eight days and now she had to look down on Planet Earth for another seventy-five days (not that she was counting), longing for her rain-soaked little cottage in Carlisle. She told him that she was going to make his life hell for the next seventy-five days and if he extended their stay any more, she would kill him. And she meant it. Pouring away his milk was the opening salvo. She had made egg, sausage, bacon, beans, mushrooms, tomatoes, toast and tea for herself, Kate and Jason.

Unusually, there was silence at the table. Kate and Jason kept glancing at each other. The spaceship was heated to a very pleasant twenty degrees, but right now it felt frosty. They had witnessed this before – all-out war between Mum and Dad. They didn't know what real war was like – they had never experienced one. But it couldn't be worse than this. Two sides out to destroy each other. It was horrible to witness. Kate and Jason finished their breakfast as soon as they could and left the table while their mum and dad glared at each other.

'We've got to do something!' Jason hissed, as soon as they were out of earshot.

They went into Kate's bedroom where she sat on the bed and started to cry. He let her get on with it. Her best ideas always came after she'd had a good cry. If he tried to comfort her, she just got angry and that was game over.

After about five minutes, she stopped and apologised. He smiled, waiting for her inspired words.

'I know!' She said, 'we'll do to them what they do to each other!'

He looked at her quizzically. He was confused.

'Mum just poured all Dad's milk away,' she said, 'because she knows he loves Chocolate Aliens. What we need to do is eject all the eggs, bacon and sausage.'

'I love bacon!' He objected. 'What will I do?'

'Do you want her to nearly kill him like she did last time?'

He shook his head.

'What then?' He asked.

'We tell her tomorrow morning when she's yelling at him.'

They hardly slept that night. They got up as soon as they heard shouting.

'What do you mean you don't know what I'm talking about!' Joanne yelled at Fred just as Kate and Jason entered the family room. Her nostrils were flaring and she looked ready to attack.

'He doesn't,' said Kate.

Joanne and Fred both turned to their children.

'He doesn't know anything about it,' said Kate.

'Doesn't know about what?' Asked Joanne, looking confused.

'You're talking about the eggs, bacon and

sausage,' said Jason. 'We ejected them yesterday.'

'Why?' Joanne yelled, even louder.

'Because we're sick of you two fighting,' Kate said calmly.

'He started it!' Joanne yelled.

It occurred to them all at the same time that the parent and child roles seemed to have reversed. With some difficulty, Joanne brought her breathing under control. But she was at a loss at what to say. Her instinct was to yell, scream, scratch, bite, punch, slap and kill.

'The rules are simple' continued Jason. 'You behave yourselves and treat each other with respect.'

It was Fred's turn to be outraged.

'How dare you speak to us like that?' He said in controlled, simmering rage.

'What do you expect us to do?' Kate said, her voice shaking. 'You nearly killed each other last time!'

Fred almost said it was Joanne who had done all that. He was just the injured party, but he realised how childish that would have sounded. Instead, he thought he could use this to his advantage. With a smile, he suggested they all sit down and talk about it.

'Dad, you're not going to use this to take advantage of Mum,' Jason said as they sat down at the table. He knew his father too well. 'And Mum, you're not going to let Dad wind you up.'

Fred and Joanne looked at each other, slightly startled.

'You should really have talked to us before you agreed to another two months,' Kate said, looking at her father. The look was more anxious than reproachful. She was scared and Fred could see that.

'I was only thinking about you. I knew that's what you wanted,' Fred said gently to his daughter.

'That's not fair, Dad,' said Jason. 'It's what *you* wanted. You knew Mum would hate it.'

'But I was thinking about you…' Fred's voice faded away weakly.

'We don't want to see you and Mum fighting. Do you know how horrible that is?' Kate asked, not daring to look at them.

Their parents looked embarrassed. They should have known better at their age.

'There are going to be two rules,' said Jason. 'Dad, have a discussion with Mum before you make any decisions that affect us all. Mum, like it or not, you're stuck here for the next two and a half months. Make the best of it and stop making our lives hell.'

Joanne looked ashamed of herself.

'If you don't, I'll leave next year,' said Jason. He would be sixteen years old then.

Both Joanne and Fred knew this was no empty threat. Jason always did what he said, no matter what the consequences.

'What will you do?' Joanne asked, unable to keep the shock out of her voice.

'That will be my problem, Mum. Not yours.'

Joanne did not want to lose her son. She knew if he left, he would never come back or even talk to them again. She looked at Fred, pleadingly. He looked at her. They knew they were beaten. But it actually felt liberating to have boundaries. It was something neither of them had ever had.

As the atmosphere lifted, they all smiled at each other and turned to look out of the window at Planet Earth. A small army of Chocolate Aliens floated past the window. They had been ejected as well.

The Battle of Strawberry Fields
Emarcian Hide

"Welcome! Welcome! You're here just in time!
You must be Lisa." A stony voice said,
"Ah! And Hercule, this will be divine!
Defending both field and strawberry bed."

Two hungover heads opened their eyes,
turning away from sun splintered light.
A patient ogre stood awaiting reply
while Hercule adjusted his snake skin tights.

"A battle you say? Right here and now?
Look here ogre we don't mean to offend,
but both of us really cannot see how,
after our twelve labours celebration weekend."

Lisa is in a lion onesie (although very cute)
and I personally think that my Hydra mankini
does not really make for a well armoured suit.
Are you sure you need us? Both Lisa and me?"

"Look here it's so tiny, this little henge..."
The ogre then stopped him, raising his hands.
Pointing he said, "It's not the henge you defend.
Beyond this gate of stones lie the Eternal Lands."

"To the Forever Fields where the strawberries grow."

With thoughtful look, twiddled tail in her hands,
Lisa exclaimed, "These berries seem vital so,
why not plant them in Elysian lands?"

The ogre laughed right down in his belly.
"You really don't know? Surely you jest!
If you wish to grow the juiciest berry,
everyone knows English soil is the best."

"Now enough! The Time for talking is done."
Held in stony grip then pulled through the gate,
"These fields need the heroes you have become.
You must go on now, before it's too late."

Confused Lisa and Hercule walked on alone,
on golden bootie and soft slippered paws.
The field lay ahead, the foe still unknown.
Both readied themselves for the strangest of wars.

Before them a field spread out acres wide.
Striped all the way down in neat green rows,
fat leafy plants grow bursting with pride,
their precious red harvest in sunlight glows.

It's hard to imagine some enemy or beast
who would do battle with fruit and butterfly.
Both stood guard over this godly feast,
when from left of the field came whimpering cries.

Brown lumps way off, you could only just see,

too small to be boar, too bold to be deer,
tumbling and crashing. "Can it possibly be?
The Labrador puppy menace is here!"

Hercule and Lisa both sprang into action,
vaulting row after row towards the first pup.
Avoiding all plants (and, of course, soil disruption).
Open armed, Lisa soon swept the first cutie up.

"No way!" exclaimed Hercule. "Now you're ahead!"
Lisa giggled and winked while flicking her tail,
with a triumphant "Ha Ha!" Hercule grabbed three
instead!
The last doggy bit him with a frustrated wail.

Heartily laughing they picked up the rest.
Labs four and twenty the pair counted out.
"It seems we prevail against this furry pest!"
Then came more yapping as they turned about.

More puppies emerged from around every bush.
Clawing and digging with mindless destruction,
strawberries were eaten or trampled to mush.
Rows turned into holes by the baby invasion.

Overwhelmed by these furries they could not stop,
where strength had failed maybe thinking would
work.
But what could save the diminishing crop?
Lisa examined two berries down in the dirt.

"These are supposed to be magical berries,
so what do they do? Should we find out?"
They both ate a fruit, apprehensive and wary.
A suffocating sensation began causing doubt,

From the ground slowly a drosophilic cloud rose.
It silently lingered, a dreaded black cloak.
But this bleak fog went the direction *they* chose,
an angry miasma swirling like smoke.

Billions of flies obeyed their command,
building a fearsome, towering plume.
They swarm to attack, but caused no real harm.
Elsweyr bells toll the puppy hoard's doom.

They rushed into ears, filled open mouths,
flying in eyes and up noses they stung.
Choking and blinded the puppy hoard routs.
With tails between legs they all turn and run.

"Heroic indeed! Well done! Thanks a bunch!"
The ogre's entrance was sudden, "Amazing! Now
Go".
"Hey wait, what, no time for lunch?
It was hungry work defeating your foe".
"True, but those berries counted as brunch,
so now time is an illusion, lunch time doubly so!"

Can You Hear
Caroline SB

Our world is noisy, full of sounds we often do not
hear
but take yourself out of the cacophony of noise
that blasts your ears.
Find the silence and stillness
within you and start to listen, really listen

through the tuneless hum of traffic, the droning
of human voices and thoughts.

Listen - maybe it's a single tweet, then a second, a
shrill from a wren, a cooing from a wood pigeon.
Don't let the bangs and slamming of life distract you
listen carefully and hear
the buzzing of the bee
even the movement of the tree
stretching, opening to life
with a silent swish
now you can really hear the important
rhythm of life.

Love Most Eternal
Ian Jarvis

Jonathan took Helena's hand and led her to the dance floor. They smiled contentedly as they faced each other. As the music began, they started their waltz. Many emotions flooded through them. They had thought this day would never come. He'd thought he would never get married. After all, immortality is not the sort of thing women looked for in a man. Fate must have been smiling on him to have found such a beautiful woman. Her face was angelic. Her golden hair cascaded down past her shoulders. Her voice was as sweet as a songbird. He felt unworthy of the love of such a remarkable woman, especially one as kind-hearted, compassionate and spirited as Helena. He could hardly believe that she wanted to marry him in both her lifetimes. He remembered the day she was poisoned in her past life two hundred and eighty-five years ago. The heartache he felt would have been too much to handle for anyone. When her past self died, he cradled her lifeless body in his arms. He thought his heart would shatter into a million pieces like fragile glass. Then to find her reincarnated in this modern time and now she too was immortal. They had all eternity together and his love for her would neither fade nor die.

Helena had danced with Jonathan before. Their first dance in her past life was very enjoyable. Their first dance in her current life was amazing. She had never been more relaxed dancing with anyone else. Their first dance as husband and wife was the sweetest moment she had ever experienced. Everything about him was warm, kind, gentle and loving. She felt like she was dancing on air.

No one could take their eyes off the happy couple. Their feelings seemed to be something that was rarely felt by two people even though it was possible to find.

My Alice
Lynne Parkin

Overton Hall was built in 1790 as the country retreat for Sir George Overton, Wool Merchant. It now stood tired, outdated, and on the outside weatherworn in places. It was last occupied by servicemen maimed in the name of King and Country on the battlefields of World War Two. The Ministry of Defence barbed wire was still serving a purpose, keeping the residents and villagers in, and the wider community out. Some patients were top secret, that was what the locals thought when it first opened in 1940.

Today, although its residents could prove otherwise, the staff were thankful that the villagers still believed it empty. It meant that no one ventured down the long-overgrown drive and the Hall was set back far enough to be inconspicuous. The owners preferred it that way. They didn't need or want the village or the rest of the country looking at them and their methods of treatment. The doctors shut themselves off from the world and the locals were better not knowing. The comings and goings of delivery men and patients were reserved for late evening, the darker the better. Listen in the quietness however and they could convince themselves that they could on occasions hear muffled speech and someone scream. Ghosts of the past? If only that were the truth….

No two days were the same at the Hall, according to the activities and treatment programmes put up on the noticeboard. Ask any of the patients and they would laugh and tell you differently, those that could anyway. Margaret, just a shell of her former self, stared blankly until there was a loud noise and she would dive inside the nearest cupboard, usually the one in the grandfather clock in the lounge. Rupert paid more attention to his voices than his peers. Joseph spoke in rhyme all the time, with a plum in his mouth and a twang from the south, the posh youth was so annoying. Ben shook every few minutes and he foamed at the mouth, it could be quite frightening to see but he was harmless enough and they were used to him by now. Rupert Cordukes, who was the illegitimate son of Prince Rainier 3rd of Monaco on certain days of the week and Winston Churchill on others, held court every day. Those that were able to form an opinion about Rupert thought he was a twerp. Lottie cried and cried and cried, apart from the days she was taken to who knows where. When she came back later that day her whole demeanour had changed, it was as though she had just arrived and didn't know anyone.

Then there was Hugh and Alice who were inseparable. If you asked Hugh, they had the kind of bond that would have you believe they were siblings. Hugh had roller-coaster emotions, up one minute, down the next, happy, sad, angry, ecstatic and anything in between. Then there was Alice, hard to fathom and mischievous. Alice was frail, her thin body showing all the signs of age for someone beyond her years, according to Hugh. The one thing they all had in common, however, was very rich influential parents who liked to keep their outward integrity intact and the family flaws hidden!

When the sun rose that morning, all was not well. The sky was green, the grass blue, the flowers were every shade of orange and their leaves were brown. The sun itself was a vibrant red. Hugh thought of Alice, with her long red hair and newly ironed pinafore. He knew she would be waiting for him because she had told him so. That's what friends did, and Alice was his friend. He pictured her sitting on the grass humming to herself, she hummed a lot, saying it took away his voices. Hugh knew that she would be waiting for him, they were going butterfly hunting. They wanted 12 to take to the cook. If he didn't turn up soon, she would have to hunt without him. Breakfast first, then adventures.

It was midday, and Hugh was still indoors having found himself grounded until teatime. You shouldn't be punished for something you hadn't done, he thought, and the incident with breakfast wasn't his fault; someone had put frog spawn in his porridge. He shuddered at the thought, or was it a silent chuckle? Not his fault, it was never *his* fault. Now here he was in the hallway wishing he was with Alice. He tried to think beyond his predicament, to think about life before, but it was hopeless. Hugh decided he would refuse lunch in protest, that was something Alice often did. Actually, she always did it and no one could tell him why. Hugh hated it when Alice refused to speak to anyone, especially to him.

'My Alice,' he whispered. 'How I miss you'

Picking up her net and jam jar, Alice headed towards the roses which were in the walled garden, one of the forbidden places. She was angry with Hugh; he was so unreliable these days. He would say *she* was unreliable. Stalemate. The gate made of oak had a metal grill in the middle and when Alice stood on tiptoe, she could see through it and spy. In amongst the roses, were butterflies of every size and colour. She quietly opened the gate and entered. Then putting the jam jar on the path, she skipped towards the rose bushes with her net. It was not the same without her best friend beside her, but knowing she was in one of Matron's forbidden areas made her heart jump. His loss, she thought. With thin tired arms, she swished her net backwards, forwards, up and down until she was in a frenzy. One by one it was filled with beautiful butterflies which she transferred to the jam jar. On the last rose, she found two plump hairy caterpillars nibbling leaves. Just what she needed and for the first time that morning she smiled. They too went into the jam jar and they nestled contently on the privet leaves at the bottom.

In the library, Hugh stood with his hands pressed against the window pane. Nothing on the outside appealed to him. The colours had now faded and it was as grey outside as it was in. So he sat on the floor with his back against the warm radiator and sighed. He needed comfort but he was in a place where none could be found. He wanted Alice. He needed her so much he thought his head would burst. She was his best. No, his only friend. They had been through so much together. He had so wanted to be with her today.

'Come on Alice, how long does it take to catch something?' Hugh shouted impatiently.

'Who are you, and who are you talking to?' An austere voice behind him asked.

Hugh turned to see Rupert complete with a royal blue cloak made from satin curtain lining, a crown made out of tin foil and a sceptre made out of what looked like a wooden spoon. He tried to stifle a laugh as he said,

'It's me, Hugh, just me, and you wouldn't believe me if I told you I was actually talking to someone else. You're just like everyone else.'

Rupert poked Hugh in the chest with his sceptre and sneered,

'You're weird you, plain and simple weird. You don't belong in my kingdom. You are not one of my subjects.'

Then with a swish of his cloak, he flounced up the hall and into the sitting room, tutting as he went.

Before Hugh could think about following him to reply the tea bell rang. Where had the afternoon gone? He was sure he was looking outside a minute ago. Hugh trudged head down into the dining room until he reached his chair. Glancing at his plate with suspicion he moved a piece of cabbage. His meal times always started with the same ritual. He raised one hand slowly and pointed with the other towards his cabbage, where two plump caterpillars were munching. He knew they would say he had done it himself; they always did. What, put the caterpillars on his own plate, why would he? He glanced around his head full of questions such as, why wasn't there a chair for Alice? Where did she go at meal times? Was she responsible for his mealtime problems?

'Where are you Alice?' he shouted. 'Why do you leave me?'

'Quiet Hugh,' Matron chided. 'You are disturbing the others with your nonsense.'

'Yes, shut up trout face, you basket case! Where's your friend, dead end?' Joseph waxed lyrical.

It was not nonsense. How many more times did he have to tell them? The more they refused to listen the stronger Alice became. As he'd missed lunch, he couldn't leave his tea because he was starving, so as soon as he had finished he would go straight to his room. Before he could do that Matron beckoned him with her pointy index finger.

'Where were you at lunchtime? We couldn't find you anywhere. In fact, you were missing most of the afternoon and we are not in the habit of running around after spoilt children who do not obey orders and decide to have a strop.'

'I was here,' Hugh insisted. 'It was Alice that wasn't.'

Matron pursed her lips and hissed, 'I have had enough of your imaginings. We'll see what Doctor

Watkins has to say tomorrow. Now out of my sight.'

Hugh didn't need telling twice. He grabbed an orange from the basket on Matron's table and ran straight upstairs. He opened the bedroom door and once inside slammed it shut. Sitting on his bed he could feel the anger rising in his blood.

'What's wrong, mate?' Alice asked.

'What do you care?' he grumbled. 'You're never here.'

'I'm here more than you think,' she said.

'Have you got a girl in your room?' Came a familiar voice from the landing.

'Get stuffed Rupert,' Hugh replied. 'Go and talk to yourself, you usually do.'

'I'll tell,' Rupert continued.

Hugh huffed and said, 'Please yourself, do what you like. No one believes me anyway. Just leave me alone!'

'Temper, temper,' Alice chided. 'You know what happens if you lose your temper. You are behaving like a big baby.'

'That's right blaming me for everything. It's never your fault, is it?' He sobbed.

It was then he spotted her jam jar on his bedside table and jumped up. He grabbed it and dangled it in front of her.

'Put it back,' Alice yelled.

'Won't,' he replied. 'Not now, not ever.' It was at that moment his anger overflowed. The colours appeared in his vision and he threw the jam jar at the wall where it smashed into hundreds of sharp pieces which scattered haphazardly across the room. In those few moments Hugh felt his mind shatter too.

Alice closed her eyes and sighed. If only Hugh could have allowed himself to believe that the jam jar was his. She knew the day was not over and tomorrow was yet to come. Alice was there for him today, as she

was the day all of his trauma began. In fact, she would
be there for Hugh as long as he needed her.

In the distance, the cook screamed.

Batman!
Emma McKenzie

I am the super-sleuth dog-walker
7:30am and I am stalking the streets
In Batman pyjamas,
With yesterday's hair
And pillow creases down one cheek;
Expertly dodging early risers,
Bin men and curtain twitchers,
It is the starlings that call me out
From the roof tops,
Wolf Whistling
In their iridescent coats,
Chirping and wheezing with laughter

Returning Home
Catherine

This story is based on a true story about my father's university friend and visits to him over time on a Scottish island. His name has been changed and the island not named explicitly but could be identified by someone familiar with Scottish islands. We haven't met many times, but he has kept contact every year by telephone – usually in the early hours of the morning!

Introduction

"Please fasten your seatbelts flight LA 32 is due to depart in two minutes." The voice of the steward, in a thick Glaswegian accent, came over the loudspeaker. Hector secured himself carefully in his seat and tried to settle himself. He closed his eyes, as final adjustments were made to the aircraft in preparation for take-off. He was relieved to find a vacant seat next to him as this meant he wouldn't be forced to talk to anyone, as had been the case on the previous flight. He wasn't unfriendly, he just needed time to think about what he was doing.

The plane began to taxi down the runway as the engines accelerated to reach their full capacity. This was the part Hector dreaded, although a frequent flyer, take-off always caused him worry; he was a naturally superstitious person. Once the plane was airborne he could relax slightly and collect his thoughts. This was a momentous journey for him. He was about to embark on a new chapter of his life.

Three years ago, Hector had left university with a degree in modern languages and after taking his accountancy exams he secured a job with an accountancy firm. His future had seemed certain and his prospects good. He'd had no hesitation in taking a long rental on a flat in an affluent area of London. Although on the surface it appeared everything was going right for him, something was missing. His father had been in the army and therefore Hector had never had one place which he could call home. After his mother's death his father had moved into a croft the family owned in a remote area of the Highlands. When Hector visited him there he had felt safe and comfortable; whereas he had never felt the same in London. He had become increasingly anxious by the stressful demands placed on him by modern day society, constantly being rushed off his feet at the will of others, and having to meet unrealistic deadlines. This wasn't him. There had been several social acquaintances, but his way of life had seemed to exclude the real friendship he had enjoyed at university. His London contacts seemed overtaken with mortgages, fast cars and money, whilst he loathed materialism and conformity and longed for a simpler life style.

Hector's thoughts were interrupted by the air hostess, who appeared at his elbow and offered him a drink. He thankfully accepted a small scotch. He enjoyed the odd glass of whisky, but he wasn't a heavy drinker. The hostess asked if he would like anything else, but he decided he would prefer to continue his reminiscences without further distraction.

He sat back and settled comfortably to regain his thoughts. It was a relief not to be restricted by his dull grey business suit and restricting choking collar and tie. From his earliest days at prep school he had hated formal wear. It had been a ritual in London, that on returning to his flat after work, he had taken off his suit and put on a pair of baggy Levis and a sloppy, holey Guernsey jersey. From now on he would be free to wear anything he chose on a daily basis.

He glanced out of the porthole, but he was unable to see anything as there was too much cloud over the sea. The last time he had been on this flight had been only three months ago, when he had managed to take time off work. That visit had decided him. His aunt had retired to the island two years before and now ran a small pottery. She specialised in designing plaques, lamps and jewellery with Celtic designs. In contrast to the suffocating smog he had left in London, the ugly grey concrete tower blocks and ceaseless traffic jams, the island appeared like another world. When he had arrived it had been pitch black, and therefore he had been unable to make out any landmarks. His aunt had met him at the airport, and they had walked to her chalet along a rough beaten track. The lights from the nearby whisky distillery and airport were the only signs of life on this mysterious island. The following morning Hector had awoken to discover this magical island and his future home.

"Please fasten your seatbelts, we will be landing shortly. We hope you had a pleasant flight and will travel with us again soon." Hector came back to the present, he felt a sudden wave of emotion but he looked out of the window and was rewarded by the sight of his beautiful mountain. Surely this was a good omen. As the plane came to a halt on the runway he felt he was coming home. He passed the control barrier and saw his friend Hamish's car skidding to a halt in the airport carpark. Although he had only met Hamish on his last visit he had felt an immediate affinity. Both had similar backgrounds and shared the same profession. As Hamish's car finally arrived at Hector's new home Hector knew he had found what he had been lacking - a place to call home.

Chapter 1
Several years later

The phone rang in the early hours - who could this be at such an unsociable hour? It turned out to be Hector, wanting to invite my dad, his old friend from university, to bring his family and stay with him in his now more habitable cottage on a Scottish island. I was about eleven at the time and my brother, Thomas, just turned eight years old.

My parents, Thomas and I set out by car from North Yorkshire, and finally travelled by ferry from the Scottish mainland. As we came into port we saw a figure waving vigorously. This was unmistakably Hector. We followed his old Volvo along the old, winding roads and beaten tracks to his cottage. On the way we saw rabbits with myxomatosis. They stared at us with their bulging eyes before retreating off into the undergrowth. I was told the disease originated in Australia as an attempt to control the rabbit population. The virus had spread rapidly. I thought it was disgusting and I felt sorry for the rabbits who stumbled about blindly.

We had already heard about Hector's cottage. It was the lodge at the entrance to a large highland estate. The castle was now derelict and unoccupied. When he had first visited his aunt, he had heard from one of her guests that the Kildare estate was advertising for a land agent. As he listened Hector had had a desire to apply for the position. He also found that the lodge was for sale. He made an appointment with the agent and went to see the property. Straight away he felt attracted to the pink quartz cottage, glistening in the weak sunlight. He overlooked the lack of any facilities. There was no electricity or mains drainage. He looked forward to developing the property. Once he had been offered the position of land agent he put in an offer for the cottage, which was accepted.

We parked alongside the isolated cottage. The evidence of ongoing building was evident from the builders materials scattered around. Downstairs several rooms were off limits, everywhere seemed untidy. The lounge had several comfy leather chairs and a sofa but were covered with cast off clothes and official looking papers. We later discovered these were old accountancy papers which Hector was using to fuel the open fire.

That evening we were treated to a hearty meal of lamb, carrots and potatoes. There was a mound of potatoes. Hector's freezer was loaded with joints of meat, these had been given to him in return for his professional accountancy services to a local farmer. Bartering it seemed was a common practice on the island rather than the exchange of money.

During the next few days we came to know and love the island. The scenery was magnificent. The only sound was the sea lapping the rocks on the shore. One particularly memorable afternoon we took Hector's dog along the coast and then up his mountain – the highest point on the island. As we neared the summit the view was breath-taking. We were just able to make out the coast of Ireland. Suddenly the sky changed dramatically from a dull shade of misty grey to patches of clear azure with wisps of white cloud. The watery sun caught the sea and was reflected on a passing boat. On our descent we were puzzled by the behaviour of Hector's rescue dog. It stopped suddenly and seemed to be staring into the distance. We followed the direction of its gaze and were rewarded by a glimpse of fallow deer frisking on the track ahead of us which lead to a nearby forest. Some slight noise disturbed them and they soon disappeared into the dappling woods. Thomas, my brother discovered a hoard of old coloured empty bottles made from thick blue and green glass. We wanted to take them home as souvenirs of our visit but Hector forbade us from doing so as he believed it would bring us bad luck. He explained that the bottles were the remnants of a party and shouldn't be disturbed. Rumours were rife about hauntings on the Kildare estate.

On our final day we set out to visit a neighbouring island to see the famous whirlpool renowned for swallowing many ships. On our car journey north Hector told us to keep a look out for Haggis, "look out for a bird which has legs of unequal length to adapt to the terrain." My brother and I thought we made some sightings but these were never confirmed. When we finally reached our destination we walked along the rugged cliffs but were disappointed as the whirlpool was not in angry mood.

That evening, after supper we all went for a walk in the grounds of the castle. It was a chilly evening with a wind causing the branches of the trees to bend and the leaves to rustle, eerily. We passed many exotic plants brought from faraway lands by a previous laird. As we rounded a bend in the path, we were confronted by the ghostly ruins of a castle. The roof had long ago caved in and vegetation had taken over. We jumped as a crashing sound came from within. Hector told us it was the old wall tiles and remnants of a huge mirror which were falling off. As we approached, we could see the interiors of the rooms which were open to the elements. A solitary door was swinging on its broken hinges. The wood panelling was weathered and rotten. The whole place now appeared in monochrome, but it was not difficult to imagine what it would have been like in its full technicoloured splendour. Some of the stonework had been removed by local farmers to repair their buildings, making the structure too dangerous to enter. Hector told us that all attempts to develop the castle had failed. There had been various schemes to turn it into a hotel or even into a holiday village. The locals all believed in the curse placed on the castle by a former laird. Fortunately, this hadn't extended to Hector's lodge!

It was with heavy hearts that the next day we left Hector and his island promising to return soon. It was to be some years before we visited again.

Night Stories
John Manby

NIGHTMARE

It was the middle of the night,
I woke with a fright,
Another bad dream,
Worried about life,
Next time you see me I may look all right,
Rest assured I've been up all night.

It was the middle of the night,
I woke with a fright,
Will this dream end,
Is there hope in sight,
Drenched in sweat I take a shower,
Keeping my noise down at this unearthly hour.

It was the middle of the night,
I woke with a fright,
Who do I talk to on this cold winters night?
Do I call doctor, Or do I call a nurse?
Either way I think they would curse.

It was the middle of the night,
I woke with a fright,
No need for the doctor,
Or for the nurse,
But can anything be done,
For this ongoing curse.

COURSE WORK (DESCRIPTION OF A GLADE)

Sunlight streams through the canopy of the forest,
Like a hundred light sabres flashing through the
leaves,
With lots of different shades of green,
The trees stand tall and firm,
Like giant sentries,
The light is blinding and constant.
Tangled nettles and ferns carpet the forest floor.

THE FIGHT

I went for a taxi, It was the end of the night,
Did I have fun at the big fight,
One of the boxers was in terrible plight,
The referee had to stop the fight,
The crowd was enraged it was to be an early night,
But what about the boxers terrible plight?
The crowd had cheered on. As the boxer went down,
His head hit the canvas with a terrible sound,
What must have been a medic rushed to the ground,
But slipped on the blood that pooled all around,
The crowd booed and hissed,
Would it have been fun if the other boxer had
missed?
The taxi pulled up,
The driver got out, then opened the door and
ushered me out.

THE MATCH

As I walk down Bootham Crescent going to the
match,
  I hear the crowd roar, I'm late, I will have to dash,
  Squeezing through the turnstile ticket in hand,
  I rush to my seat, I`m in the family stand.

No score yet, I've not missed much,
  As a player runs by, then gets tripped up,
  The ref blows his whistle long and hard,
  Then searches his pocket for another card.

Half time already, time for a brew,
  I`d better rush to get in the queue,
  Back in my seat the players run out,
  While the manager takes his place in the dugout.

The whistle blows. The action starts,
  Players running round in fits and starts,
  A shot. A goal. We take the lead,
  That will help us up the league.

The floodlights come on. As it starts to get dark,
  We score again, we're playing them off the park,
  The fans start singing their favourite songs,
  Come on City let's have another one.

The Talisman
Angi

It was just a pebble on the beach; one of thousands
marking the high tide line, yet there was something
about it that called out to her. Something that caused
her to stop, stoop and pick it up with barely a pause in
her lonely walk along the shingle hinterland between
land and sea. The small, oval stone with a neat hole
in one quarter fitted comfortably in the palm of her
hand. Its milky-white surface was as rough as her
man's chin come eventide. The thought conjured
bittersweet memories of her hand caressing his cheek,
the feel of the coarse stubble beneath her fingers as she
wondered not for the first time why he didn't just stop
fighting what Nature intended and grow a beard ;like
the other men in the village.

The Village. Perhaps she should go back.
She'd walked further than normal in the grey misty
gloom that heralded sunrise. She'd even outdistanced
the all-pervasive oily wood perfume of the village
smoke house. Full light would bring out the
inshoremen readying their boats, nets and lobsterpots
for the turning tide and she had no desire to be seen
People thought her odd enough already.

Turning into the strengthening wind
accompanying the fast incoming tide she caught
snatches of a faint otherworldly melody blending and
contrasting with the constant murmuring of wave on
shingle; a song without words that filled her with a
desolate yearning for home. As though in sync with
her innermost thoughts, random gusts of sea spray
peppered her exposed face with stinging salty drops,
blurring her vision with tears she could not herself

shed.

Across the bay an elderly fisherman seated on a pile of old crates sipped hot strong black tea from a chipped enamel mug. Wincing slightly at the blistering heat and bitter taste, he listened to the hauntingly beautiful seal song drifting across the water. The music enhanced these precious moments of peace before the long day's fishing that lay ahead. A time he'd become accustomed to taking for himself since his wife's passing a few years back.

Glancing over the rim of his mug his still keen eyes caught sight of his daughter-in-law, a pale, grey cloaked apparition materialising in the cold grey dawn, gliding towards the tiny stone cottage on the headland she and his son shared. Even from this distance her loneliness was tangible. Sympathy washed over his age worn leathery face. She seemed so lost, so distant, vulnerable. He wanted to give comfort and ease her burden of grief but had no idea how to approach her. If only his son could witness the love she still bore him, even now, how much she missed him. So poignantly obvious in these melancholy walks he'd often seen her take at the margins between day and night, frequently as now to the accompaniment of seal song.

Thinking back, she'd always been a loner, somehow always on the margins of the small fishing community with its stone cottages and communal buildings huddled together behind the sheltering embrace of thick harbour walls. Perhaps because she was a foundling – found by himself and his brother one wintery dawn after a ferocious overnight storm. She'd been not much more than a bairn then. In a tattered grey cloak with her scraggy long hair knotted with seaweed she seemed like some lost mermaid of legend.

Randomly his then young son had taken the lacings from the neckline of his shirt to tie the watery, dark mass from her face as they carried her to the warmth and safety of his brother's cot. In retrospect it was as if this random act of kindness had bound her to him, for whenever possible she'd follow his son around; a devoted puppy chasing her master. Her quiet, timid nature being at odds with the more boisterous village children, who whilst not unkind to her, found her strange and thus frequently left her to her own devices, so that his son who often neglected her was perhaps her only friend. Over time her friendly devotion increased and in due course they'd married.

Perhaps if they'd had children she'd have been less alone but that blessing had been denied them. She had, after some years conceived but the child hadn't lived long enough to draw breath. Tragically infant mortality and stillbirth was not uncommon, however the inability of his son and daughter-in-law to cope with, and reconcile over their shared loss was unusual.

In theory, she'd still been young enough to bear more children but after the tragedy his son had ceased working with him, instead signing onto the crew of the community's one deep sea fishing vessel. Unable to bear the company of his wife for more than a few days unresolved grief had driven him to seek solace on the sea.

Being childless and all but abandoned by her man for days at a time had set his daughter-in-law even further apart from the other womenfolk, who, like he felt sorry for her but knew not what to say.

It wasn't that his son didn't care. The old man could see how deeply he mourned his child, but had internalised his grief to the extent that he'd become blind to his wife's pain, trapping them both in separate lobster pots of intense misery and grief. Neither of them knowing how to reach out and comfort the other or how to support and move forward together.

Cold, hungry and exhausted, he stood a moment shrouded in darkness just beyond the golden glow of the cottage window. The frosty air nipped at exposed skin and made wispy alcohol-soaked clouds of his breath. He needed time to steel himself for the silent censure that awaited him within. Not that he didn't deserve it. The fishing vessel had docked hours ago and once they'd landed the catch he'd gone to the tavern with his crewmates. Celebrating their good fortune or drowning his sorrows? He wasn't even sure which anymore, probably both. But to hell with it! Why couldn't his woman be angry, shouting her disapproval like all the other fishwives? Showing him some damned emotion for once. Eventually his rumbling stomach drove him across the threshold.

Inside was his woman, her tempestuous, dark hair bound at the neck with that cord he'd given her all those years ago, its ends as frayed and worn as their relationship had become. With her back to the rosy, crackling log fire in the hearth, she sat at the table deftly darning a sock in the warm glow of the brass and glass lamp. A neatly folded pile beside her showed she'd been at this activity for some time.

She startled at the cold draught that accompanied him into the warmth. This domestic scene irritated him but he was perversely pleased to have discomforted her no matter how briefly. Ignoring her quiet greeting he slammed the door before seating himself at the table eagerly awaiting the fish stew, whose aroma alone was enough to make his mouth water.

The swift arrival of the anticipated hearty dish and accompanying mug of ale pacified him, at least for the time being. Eagerly he took a mouthful savouring the slight saltiness and the combined textures of fish, vegetables and edible seaweeds whilst cursing its heat for burning his tongue. At least the woman could cook. This was far superior to the bland fare he'd eaten at the tavern hours ago now. To be fair she'd always been a competent, dutiful wife in all ways except the only one that mattered to him – giving him a family. Taking a swig of ale he was aware of her watching him with calm composure from the high-backed wooden chair beside the inglenook.

Alcohol fuelled disgust surged in him. How could she be so calm, so inhuman? The sooner he was away from her the better. "Get my kit ready for first light. I'm out with the morning tide." He hadn't intended going out again this close to Winter but the boat's new owner wanted to take advantage of the unseasonably calm weather they'd been having and was offering higher wages and a share of the catch . . He hadn't signed on yet but a fisherman of his experience would always be welcome. Not that he'd bother telling her that.

"Must you go? It's madness to even think about it. This weather won't last more than a day, two at the most before the storms come". Again so bloody calm. Her weather sense had always been spot on. Somewhere deep within his consciousness a tiny voice of reason, quiet, like hers pleaded with him to listen, but with senses dulled by drink it was easy to ignore it.

She was on her feet a tentative hand reaching across the table towards him. Reaching out but hovering just above his hand, unable to touch him. Not that he wanted the unwelcome intrusion into his private hell.

"Like I haven't weathered storms before!" He snorted. "Besides should Davy Jones claim me it'll be a blessing. I'll be free and you can go back to wherever the hell you came from!"

With a sharp intake of breath her hand recoiled as though burned. Finally a reaction from her! This was what he wanted wasn't it? So why then was there a taste in his mouth like sour beer? No longer hungry, he rose abruptly pushing aside the half eaten stew and turned towards their bedroom at the rear of the house. "I've said I'm going. That's an end to it"

Stunned as though his words had dealt her a physical blow, she watched the bowl fall to the flagstone floor, spewing contents and shattering into pieces. The crash broke the spell. Her words sounded little more than the distant roar of the waves as she voiced the question she wasn't sure she wanted answering. "You wish to set me free?"

He stopped before the door, his hand about to turn the knob, his back towards her "Go. Go if that's what you want. I'm going to bed. I'll be out at first light."

"Wait." Swiftly she freed her hair, removing the cord, the first thing he'd ever given her. The cord that she'd bound her hair or worn around her neck like a collar ever since. Not a day had gone by when it hadn't been with her . . . until now. Retrieving the pebble she'd found only that morning, but which now seemed a lifetime ago she threaded the cord through the hole to create a pendant; a lover's charm against misfortune. "If you've given your word, then you must go. But take this; my farewell gift to you. This stone is of the land. It has survived the sea and returned to the land. May it's subtle magic be a talisman to bring you back safe to those who love you. May it also serve to remind you of me when I am gone and of my love for you."

This response surprised him. Out of curiosity and suddenly sober he turned to face her, seeing her for the first time in years. Dark shadows underscored her eyes. Evidence if any were needed of restless nights haunted by dreams. Her eyes themselves dark fathomless depths, as soulless and empty as his own. She was thin too. Didn't she take care of herself in his absence? He'd always assumed her to be care free, untouched by their shared tragedy since he always returned to an immaculately tidy house, with some completed knitting; socks, hat or thick jumper waiting for him, and hot food whatever time of day or night he turned up. Guiltily, no longer able to face her he glanced to the spilled, broken mess on the floor, then back to her outstretched arm and the talisman – a small white stone suspended on his old cord.

Unlike many who made their living on the sea, he'd never been superstitious. Nor did he hold with religion either. If anything he was a fatalist; what was going to happen would happen regardless of whatever you believed or tried to do to change it. His first impulse was to laugh, ridicule and refuse her offer, but . . . there had been something poignant about it. Avoiding her gaze he took the offered gift and retired without a word, for there was too much to say now that it was too late.

Wind driven waves had crashed into and over the harbour walls, causing damage to several small boats moored within, but the village had been spared the onslaught. The buildings on the headland had been less fortunate, the constantly pounding waves had cause a landslip taking most of an old stone cottage and the few disued storage sheds with it. Thankfully no one in the village was hurt but everyone turned a watchful eye seawards. Praying for the safe return of the fishing vessel and its crew of six who'd set out for the deep sea mere hours before the worst storm in decades hit.

They were about to call off the search when his father found him washed ashore close to the rocky outcrop at the far end of the bay. He was badly injured, unconscious but alive . . .just, unlike the other three men nearby. His left hand tightly clasped around some small object suspended from his neck. Clearly some lover's token, which confused the fishing community since he'd always preferred a life at sea to matrimony and by their reckoning had never had a lover.

It took months for his body to heal. True he'd lost his right leg below the knee but was able to walk slowly with the aid of a wooden prosthetic and stick. Otherwise he was a changed man, no longer going out fishing he filled his days sat mending nets outside the harbour front cottage he shared with his father. However at dawn and dusk, when tides and weather permitted he'd taken to going for long walks along the beach losing himself in the haunting melody of seal song. Seeking solitude and an outlet for the inconsolable grief over some unknown loss was always with him. He still wore the talisman that he believed had saved his life, although where or how he came by it he had no idea, but he believed it was the key to his grief.

Sometimes if the light was right, a lone female grey seal could be seen just beyond the breakers. Should anyone be paying particular notice, it might look as though she watched the man's progress, with spray from the breaking waves peppering her face with salty tears she could not herself shed.

Submission Guidelines
Alex Weston

"We're sorry for the delay to this Virgin East Coast service which has been caused by a signalling fault between Darlington and Durham." People shifted in their seats, made eye contact with their neighbours. Unaware, the voice continued, "We are hoping to be able to continue very shortly and will keep you informed of developments."

"Which means they don't have a bloody clue," the man opposite Sally said. She'd been avoiding looking at him since she'd got on the train in York. A couple of quick glances as she'd slid into her seat had revealed that he was remarkably good looking in a better as he got older, George Clooney kind of way. But now he'd spoken to her it would be rude not to at least glance at him.

"Probably," she said. His eyes met hers and she hastily looked down. They were amazingly blue, far too attractive. The kind of eyes that made a woman forget she didn't need a man in her life.

"Any idea where we are?"

The lights from the carriage were reflected in the glass and the raindrops streaking the window. Behind that was unremitting blackness. "Somewhere in the wilds of County Durham, I'd say. Darlington was the last station we went through."

"Oh." He shrugged with a half-smile. "Doesn't mean much to me, I'm afraid. Are we far from Newcastle?" He pronounced it as two words with an entirely unnecessary R in the second syllable.

"About another twenty-five minutes. Once the train gets moving again, that is."

"Thanks. You going far?"

"Durham." When he looked at her blankly, she added, "It's about ten minutes from here."

"I'm sorry, I'm using you as a walking timetable." He smiled, the corners of his eyes crinkling. "I'm Guy by the way."

His hand stretched out across the table. Returning the smile, she took it. "Sally."

"Pleased to meet you, Sally. What are you doing on this benighted train on a wet evening in November?"

"I've been to a meeting in York and I'm on my way home."

"To Durham?"

"That's right. And what brings you north?"

"I'm going to Newcastle University to speak to some students."

"What about?" He was easy to talk to, easier than she'd expected from his smart silk tie and shiny cufflinks.

"Publishing. Or rather, how to get published. That's all they really want to know from me."

Sally's eyebrows rose. "You're a publisher?"

"I'm an editor. I run a general fiction list. I'm going to speak to the Creative Writing MA students in Newcastle."

"Oh." Sally swallowed. "Who do you work for?"

Don't let it be. It couldn't possibly be the company responsible for yesterday's rejection. The world wasn't that small.

"Etcetera Press."

"Oh." Not that one then. One she was still waiting to hear from nearly six months after she'd submitted.

Guy frowned. "You know them?"

"You could say that." Glancing out of the window, Sally saw a distorted reflection of her face frowning back at her. Should she? It was hardly professional. But then were publishers professional? If they were they'd reply to submissions and send something more than standard two line rejections. "I submitted my novel to your company. I'm still waiting to hear back from them."

"I see." His body language said everything as he slumped in his seat, arms crossed. "Do you have an agent?" His tone was cooler too. The warmth that had drawn her in abruptly gone.

"No. Do you have any idea how hard it is for someone like me to get an agent? I don't have contacts or friends in the right places. I'm a single mum from County Durham who just wants to write stories. And if you need an agent to get considered then why do you say you take unsolicited submissions?" Aware that the couple across the aisle were staring at her, she added more quietly, "It just pisses me off that there's one rule for the famous, that if I hosted a chat show or was a blinking supermodel I'd have no problem getting published. And one rule for everyone else like me."

"I…" Guy leaned forward, his hands clasped on the table between them.

"I'm sorry, I shouldn't have said that." Heat crept into Sally's face. "I got another rejection yesterday. A two line email that made it blindingly obvious no one had actually read my manuscript. I guess, I'm just feeling a bit sensitive about the whole thing."

"If it helps, the books by supermodels are almost always utter crap."

"It doesn't really but thanks." Forcing a half smile, she was caught again by the sheer unexpectedness of his eyes. Like bluebells. Far too blue for her peace of mind. Good job that when she got off this train she'd never see him again. He'd be only a memory and maybe, when she got over the embarrassment of her little outburst, she'd gift those eyes to the hero of her next novel.

"Any refreshments?" The steward awkwardly tugged his trolley into their line of sight. "Sir? Madam?"

"What kind of wine have you got?" Guy said.

"Red, white and rosé, sir."

"I'll risk the red." As the steward placed the small bottle and a plastic glass on the table, Guy asked, "Can I get you anything?"

Automatically, Sally shook her head. Talking to a stranger, albeit a very attractive one, on the train was one thing. Accepting a drink from him was quite another.

"It's alright, it's on expenses. Might as well get something out of Etcetera Press." There was a challenge in his grin, a dare to meet him halfway.

"In that case, I'll have two bottles of the white. Thank you."

The steward glanced between them, frowning slightly.

"And two bottles of your most expensive white for the lady," Guy said as if he were ordering in the swankiest restaurant in London.

"We only have the Reserve Alexis Lichine," the steward said. "Unless you want the Prosecco?"

"The white will be fine, thank you." As the two bottles were placed in front of her, each on a small white napkin, warmth crept up Sally's cheeks again. "Is this really on expenses?"

"Absolutely. Publishing might not run to first class travel these days but it can afford to lubricate second class with a few drinks."

"Then thank you. I was joking about two bottles though." To avoid looking like a woman with a serious drink problem she slid the second one into her handbag.

"I know." That smile again, held slightly longer

this time. By the time he glanced away, Sally felt slightly breathless. "What's your novel called?"

"*Under A Bitter Sun.*" Opening the wine, Sally took a tentative sip and was surprised to find it wasn't bad at all.

"Good title." There was slight surprise, an almost grudging respect in his voice.

"Thanks. It's a historical romance set in Darwin during the Second World War."

"What made you want to write about that?"

"I lived in Australia for two years when I was younger. Spent six months in Darwin working in a care home. One of the guys I looked after had lived through the Battle of Darwin, as they call it. He was in the Air Force and met his wife while he was stationed there. They were separated after the bombing and he didn't see her again until the end of the war."

"It's your first novel?"

"First completed novel. I've started plenty but never finished anything before."

"The Second World War is always popular. When did you submit it?"

"May. Your website says you'll get back to people within three months but I've not heard anything at all." Taking another sip of wine, Sally felt the slightly acidic tang cut through her remaining reservations. "Does anyone actually read unagented manuscripts because it sure as hell doesn't feel like it?"

Guy straightened his cufflinks. "I hope the MA students don't give me as hard a time as you."

"Have they actually submitted anything yet?"

"Probably not."

"Then you'll be fine. It's only when you've been through the process that you end up as jaded as me."

"I'll probably regret this when I get back to London but what's your surname?"

"Webster."

Scribbling her name and the title of her book on the corner of his newspaper, he said, "Well then, Sally Webster, I will find out where your manuscript is and personally make sure someone reads it."

"That's very kind of you, thank you." She should shut up now, graciously accept what he'd offered. It was more than she could possibly have hoped for. Not that reading it meant that they'd publish it but it was a start, wasn't it? A huge step forward from being adrift in the slush pile. But she couldn't let it go. She wasn't that kind of person. "But what about the writers who don't happen to bump into editors on a train? Don't they deserve to have their manuscripts read too? I just don't understand why you say you'll read all submissions when you so clearly don't."

Guy ran his hand over his face. "You're in danger of shooting the messenger, Sally Webster."

"I know. And you're a messenger bearing gifts-" her gesture took in both the wine and the scribbled words on his newspaper "-to completely mangle a metaphor. But *I* never get the chance to meet people like you. I don't have the time to do an MA or the money to go on fancy writing weekends. But that doesn't mean I can't write. I could be the next Philippa Gregory for all you know."

"Are you the next Philippa Gregory?"

"Probably not but that's not the point. The point is that you'd be missing me if I was."

"Unless I met you on a train."

The train juddered erratically before lurching forward. Sally kept a tight grip on her plastic glass but the wine bottle wobbled and fell. Her hand shot forward to grab it. Guy's did the same. Their hands collided as the bottle rolled beneath them.

"I'm so sorry," Guy said.

"No, it's my fault." There'd been a moment, a split second really, when their fingers had touched. And, in that miniscule speck of time, she'd felt something she'd long convinced herself happened only in fiction.

The tannoy crackled and the conductor's disinterested voice said, "We apologise for the delay to your journey today. This service is now running approximately fifteen minutes late."

"You shouldn't be too late for the students."

"I'm becoming less and less interested in the students." He leaned across the table. "What do you do, Sally Webster, when you're not berating editors on trains?"

There was something about the way he kept repeating her name, as if by giving it to him she'd bestowed a gift, that created an intimacy between them. "I'm a social worker."

"Good God!" His eyebrows shot up. "No wonder you have no patience with us poor publishers."

Taking a long, slow sip of wine, Sally took a second to savour his surprise. "You're not poor. At least, not in the way I deal with every day."

He was silent for a long moment before his eyes met hers. "You said you have children?"

"A daughter. Maddie. She's twelve."

"How on earth do you find time to write?"

"I find time because I have to. Because I'm happier, more alive when I write."

He nodded. "That's the best reason, the only reason really, to write."

The train slowed. Sally slid her arms into the sleeves of her coat, slugged back the last of her wine. "I get off here."

"Durham."

"Yes." Getting to her feet she picked up her bag and, when she straightened, was surprised to see him standing too.

"It's been a great pleasure to meet you, Sally Webster." His hand reached for hers and held it a second, and then another, longer than necessary.

"And you. And I hope I didn't give you too hard a time."

"Nothing that wasn't deserved. Have a good evening."

"Thanks." She had to go. The train had stopped. People where shuffling into the aisle, waiting for her to move. "Goodbye."

He smiled again as she turned. Eyes too blue.

Much later that evening, when she was clearing up from dinner and trying to help Maddie with her maths homework, her mobile pinged. A tweet. She was on Twitter but she hardly used it.

From @GuyParker01 – '@sallywebsterwrites Have dinner with me tomorrow night?'

How had he found her? And dinner? Why did he want to have dinner? All she'd done was argue with him. But he was attractive, really attractive. And he'd promised to find her manuscript. What harm could one dinner do?

"Mum?" Maddie said. "I don't get this one. It's got decimals in it."

But it would never work. He was London through and through. Their lives could never fit. Before she thought about it any more she typed,

'@guyparker01 Thank you for your request/submission. It is under consideration and I will get back to you within 3 months!'

Then putting her phone down, she sat beside her daughter and tried to focus on Key Stage 3 multiplication.

Connected
Ruth Middleton

I ask the window cleaner

In for a cup of tea.

It is hard to get the words out, they stick in my
throat,

Harsh, clipped, devoid of decoration or feeling.

I don't need to hear his refusal.

I can see it in his eyes as he edges away,

Begins to turn his back.

I fumble in my purse

Find a crisp £10 note.

I catch sight of myself in the ornate,

Gilt edged hallway mirror.

Despite the dust my reflection is bright.

Wild, uncombed hair frames my long pale face.

Drugged irises, in sticky, sleep encrusted eyes.

Three day old pyjamas,

Food splattered on my collar,

Cigarette burnt slippers.

He reaches for my money and for a moment

We are connected.

Holding on to each other through the Queens head.

It is almost enough.

I can go back to bed content, less alone.

The windows will need to be cleaned again in six
weeks time.

Seven Stray Thoughts
Michael Fairclough

Mipsey and Momo were very excited
There were dozens of seagulls, too many to be counted
The weather was sad, but it was ok
As they got to go on a boat today
Their bags were packed, they said their goodbyes
Momo brought his favourite ball, and Mipsey a pork pie
Then before they knew it, it was their turn
They were off to war, with ammo to burn

Hey hey hey, bark bark bark
You yes you, you look smart
Do you need a hairdryer or double-glazing?
How about your driveway, does it need paving?
I will mark your territory just walk me about
Sign this contract, I can start right now
Use this coupon get half off, limited time offer dog years go fast

Help as I'm hauled out of bed by the heathens
Under the coolside, I'm falling as I'm leaving
Through a rabbit hole to a trippy funky world
Where Alice gets the best of me
Teeth rip apart the flesh of me,
See this human demon's making me irate
Too late, too bad, irate I had, fallen fresh
But not for my own good, see juice is blood
For an apple in wonderland, but in human hands it's hell

Five qualities of animals I would like to have
The nose of a dog to increase my senses
The legs of a kangaroo for exits
The horn of a rhino because why not?
The agility of a cat as I have none
And lastly a snail trail so I can see where I have
beeeeeeeeeeeeeeeeeeeeeeeen

My nana had a field, full of bushes and trees
There were many in it, lots of different breeds
An apple tree, a pear tree and a conker one too
But there was one that was my favourite, but I never knew who
As when the wind blew and caught it by its branches
It would make a noise rather like flatulence, The Farting Tree

Guess your weight? What's your mass?
Would you like help finding a plant?
To hug, cuddle up to, it's good for you and free too
You seem sturdy, straddle a tree? You seem confused staring at me
I'm here to help, here for health
Government sanctioned with an environmental mantle
I wear it with leaves and such berries and nuts
I have ferrets down my trousers

When my brother disappeared, I had never seen a body
These days they're everywhere, in the dozens unfortunately
But what's truly horrid is they also steal our young
Our only clue their calling card, finger licking good

The Mystery of the Chapel
Elizabeth McLoughlin

As I walked up to the old chapel, I stood and gasped. Such beauty, the doors were so old, crafted well with carved brick work surrounding them. Such detail! I wondered how many years or centuries they had been there. What stories they could tell if only this place could talk? Who had entered this place?

It was intriguing. Curiosity had the better of me. This beautiful chapel seemed to hold so many mysteries. I opened the doors with great excitement. The smell was so old. Coming from the inside of the building, an old lady walked up to me. She was dressed as if she should have lived a few centuries ago; long black dress that was a bit puffed out, black ankle boots with studs up each side and laces that criss-crossed, a veil made with lace. Her face was very stern looking. She must have been in her eighties at least.

As I gazed upon her, I felt a bit frightened. Why was she staring at me in this way? Who is she? My gaze dropped and I took a deep breath before going to speak to her. I felt quite nervous as I raised my head again. She'd disappeared. WHAT? But where did she go? She couldn't have walked that fast and the corridor seemed very long. She wasn't sitting in the pews. She disappeared in seconds. That all seemed very strange and bit mysterious.

Anyway, I felt relieved she had gone as she scared me a bit. I dismissed the whole experience and walked about admiring the beauty of the building. Other people were in the chapel, some sitting, some walking about.

There were a couple of rooms at the far end of the chapel. Two of the rooms you were allowed to enter and one was not open to the public. I entered the first room. A sense of peace overwhelmed me. The furniture was so old, very worn and fusty smelling. This room obviously didn't get aired very often but such a peace in the room, happy contented feelings. There were some beautiful tapestries on the walls, an old table in the centre of the room. It was laid with beautiful china cups and saucers and a teapot. The spoons were real silver and well used. A lovely old-fashioned fireplace. I imagined what it would be like with a real blazing fire in this room, the heat. Warm feelings overwhelmed me. I could see and feel lots of happy feelings surrounding this room. It must have been used for entertaining.

I left and went to turn the handle on the next room. As I grasped the door handle, which was as big as my hand, it was as if I was holding ice. It was so cold. Shivers ran through me. I hesitated for a bit and then opened the door with great difficulty. A very heavy creaky door.

As I opened the door, the smell was much stronger than the room before. Old, mouldy and very cold. Should I just leave? No, I was too curious to leave. I noticed the curtains on the windows. They were very worn. The long tassels attached to them seemed to have pieces missing. I think the original colour should have been deep burgundy with gold tassels. A couple of settees which you wouldn't dream of sitting on. I touched them. They were quite shaky and worn but seemed to have had stunning patterns on them which were also worn.

Gazing around I noticed some old pictures on the walls; portraits of people belonging to the building, families and workers, different generations of people. To see the difference in the appearance and clothes of the people in the portraits was interesting. Some were from 1837 onwards. As I walked around looking at the different people on the wall and reading the plaques that were below each picture, I started wondering what these people would have been like. What was their story in life? My brain was doing overtime. On the last wall was a rather large portrait. I looked upon it and to my amazement I realised this portrait was the double of the old lady I'd seen walking towards me in the chapel. How could this be? There was no plaque below this picture. I honestly felt her eyes stare right through me. A coldness ran through my veins. As I stood wondering how this could be, I felt a hand or something touch me.

Samantha's Incident
Leanne Cairns

Samantha is a normal girl, a normal girl with two differences. One is that she is disabled and the other is that she happens to be third in line to the Kingdom of England.

Her father is Prince Christoph and her mother Deborah. Deborah is not of royal heritage, she's from Chapelfields so she is a chappy lass. Her mother and father met 15 years ago at a university function. Her disability is called hydrocephalus and cerebral palsy which reduces her ability to walk so she uses an electric wheelchair. These disabilities are life long and along with her royal duties she has learned to accomplish them with ease.

One day, as the family were going to an important function Samantha's chair stopped working. A way had to be found for her to accompany her parents. So the footmen tied a manual chair to the back of the carriage and off they went. Thirty minutes into the journey strange noises started to appear from the wheelchair and suddenly the rope snapped and Samantha was left in the middle of the road whilst her Mom and Dad trotted happily away.

It was a while before they noticed Princess Samantha was no longer with them.

"Oh no" exclaimed Prince Christoph.

"If the papers see this they will have a field day" screeched Deborah.

"Quick" ordered Prince Christoph to his bewildered footmen, Larry and Harry.

Larry and Harry scurried to gather Princess Samantha up as quickly as they could. In a flurry of skirts and crooked tiara Princess Samantha slowly regained her composure.

Two hours later, after they had received many irate phone calls from the function, off they went.

Uncommon Fledgling
Llykaell Dert-Ethrae

Illarien, Year 734

*"Regarding my reasons for choosing to give this gift…
Well, for one, you're uncommonly intelligent. Another is
your drive to achieve your passions. I also admire your
strength of character. The most important one is not
something I can adequately put into words…"*

Ah, that last part really did sound like I don't know
why I chose her. To some degree, this is true, yet from
the moment I noticed her, sat in the library doing what
she does best, I could tell she was special… Hard to
think all that was just a few weeks ago. So much has
happened since then. I'd like to think it all turned out
for the best. As it is with us, time will undoubtedly tell.

I had certainly not intended upon converting
anyone at the time I passed through Salaraq, nor had
I ever before for that matter. After my loss… it was
hardly on my list of things to even ponder, let alone
carry out, despite numerous, and often obnoxious,
requests. However, there was something about
Cinthia that I could not help but feel intrigued by.
Well, several things in point of fact. Upon her request
to know why I chose her, I was more than happy to
respond in full, detailing as much as I could as to why
I thought she would make a good Vampire.

As Cinthia was understandably cautious of me
and my motives, I was as open and honest with her as
possible. I told my Fledgling-to-be that I found her to
be a beautiful individual, full of passion, confidence,
compassion, and just the right amount of fire in her
veins to make her… well, rather a lot more exciting

than myself, that's for sure. And her forthright demeanour towards... all things physical, now that is something I certainly admire in her: it's not something I'd normally desire to partake in and so, as she's definitely more brave than I in those matters, I am in awe of her sheer confidence. Cinthia's a wholly dedicated young lady, throwing herself with every effort at all things pertaining to her chosen subject of archaeology. I recall her almost literally pouncing on me when I told her I lived at the time of the Ancients! Ha! Her enthusiasm is... invigorating. Contagious even. Which is why I entrusted her with one of my many great secrets. I'd been carrying that one around for centuries – it was time it fell into better and more appreciative hands.

I also explained to Cinthia that I was choosing her for the very reason she is not an Interist. Every other Vampire thus far has been devoted to our god, but not Cinthia. She acknowledges Its existence, but holds no opinion one way or another about It. She was therefore chosen because I feel the very fact she is external to the rest of us will lend a singular perspective on not just the Elders but the entire Vampire species. In short, I believe she will become an invaluable asset in balancing the Council's decisions.

Cinthia was – I should say *is* – entirely determined to use her new powers to pursue her career as a discoverer of lost history. This was not just fascinating from the point of view of watching her so heartily discuss her passion, but also for the fact she was not interested in the slightest in possessing or utilising her Cors for any other path than her vocation. I must admit this was deeply touching and refreshing to see and was yet another reason I desired to convert her. That has not altered and I hold no regrets on making her, however... I do regret not informing her more on her Cors and how to control and hone them. I taught her a few briefly, such as how to run, feed, form a Shield and forge a Black Flame, but all with limited and minimal success – admittedly at her newborn stage this is not outside recognised norms. However, I failed to even mention the future-telling Seer Cor and offensive summoning of stakes and I know she would have appreciated more time going over both the Cloak Cor and how to feed! She was understandably ired about that. I… am *truly* sorry I didn't have more time. Additionally, in retrospect, I realise just how inconsiderate it was to convert and not fully warn someone who has faced adversity and discrimination their entire life of the enormous level of negativity many members of the public hold against our kind. I admit, that is partially because I briefly went over that as well as my being aware that she is clever and so I assumed she already knew more… but I feel I should have done more - I should have told the extent of their bias. Dammit! There is so much more I could have done for her if only I'd… *had more time*. Surely I could have waited and gone back at some point… though there's no way of truly knowing if my Ambassadorial duties would have even allowed for it. I am uncomfortable using that as an excuse. At least she knows this and we parted on rather amiable terms… I am not ashamed to confess that I really hope to see her again. And if *anyone* fucks with my Fledgling, I *swear*…! Wait! Is *this* what being a mother is like? I genuinely never saw this for myself. Never did I even think I would… not after what happened all those years ago. Still, I am glad I made her, even though my decision was rushed. She is truly… unique. And I know she is more than capable of taking care of herself. Even so… I should have done more.

I'm also immensely relieved I didn't kill her! Damn… when her eyes glazed over after I drained her and fed her my own blood… I was terrified I'd botched the conversion! Yet just when panic was about to set in, she came back and bolted upright so fast she broke my nose. Ha! Had I not been overwhelmed with relief over her being 'alive' I doubtlessly would have burst out laughing! Cinthia then took to her new gifts with a thrill I'd not seen in another individual in decades. Her face… it was so beautiful how it glowed with delight at how freeing the experience was for her – to be able to run so fast and see things in all their heightened detail. Granted she tripped, fell and set herself on fire, but she loved every moment!… with the exception of the involuntary immolation of course – she was somewhat irked by that but she dealt with the knowledge that she would have to be careful with her velocities surprisingly well. When I told Cinthia there was so much more to learn, she just said, "Bring it on". Damn… she is really something. I *truly* cannot wait to see what kind of Vampire she becomes.

things I tried to say
CF

my heart
  has but one
     loyalty

and does
  not beat
     outside my body

Toy Town
Amy Stewart

If you cracked open my skull, you'd find a map imprinted on the inside. A tattoo on the dark bone. It's a map – a map of the tiny town that made me. When my thoughts go walking, they go there, following the same route every time.

The Garden

I was lucky in that my early years were flooded with magic. I wove my days with charms. I made potions in the bathroom with toothpaste and perfume, painted seashells with glittery nail varnish, called the wind *Hallé* and listened to her sing at night.

My entire world was the back garden – aged five, I needed nothing else. It was separated from the hill behind it by a line of conifers and a fence, which was cut lower in one place so you could jump over it with the dog. From there, the grass sloped steeply downwards to a stone wall and a pond. I used to tiptoe over the flagstones around the water, always jumping over the one I knew was wobbly.

Was there a swing tied to the thick branches of the tree by the garage, or am I just imagining that now? The earthy smell of tomatoes still takes me back to sitting in the greenhouse – sweating on the tiles, squinting at the sun through muddy panes.

We'd have fireworks in the garden every Bonfire Night. Dad would pick up a long rectangle box with explosions on the front from JTF. Catherine Wheels and Firecrackers and Roman Candles. *Danger – do not use unsupervised.* For some reason, the soundtrack from Titanic was always on, which now makes me smile to think my parents were trying to add drama to the scene. We'd huddle on the patio in gloves and hats and watch as Dad ran like a mad thing to and from where he'd speared a firework in the ground. Mum was laughing so I knew we must have been safe, but I'd always breathe out when he made it back to us in one piece.

The fireworks burst upward with a shrieking pop, showering us with fizzing sparks. The smoke always made the garden look different – it changed the shadows, the corners. I imagined hidden things crawling toward me with outstretched arms. But then everyone would clap and Dad would say, that was the best one yet.

I felt that the whole world would always be in the garden, and that the garden would always be mine. I saw the explosions of colour against the sky, not the dying of the sparks as they always, inevitably, fell.

The Dirt Path

Where the fields ran out and the houses started, there was a wide gravel path. At the other end – it wasn't very long, a hundred paces, two hundred fairy steps – was the town's main road. I got run over there, stood right back up without a bruise. But that's a different story.

The path was full of craters, full when it rained, desert-like the rest of the time. It was a craggy, prehistoric landscape that looked different every time you walked it.

I used to see shapes in the stones at my feet; make mythologies out of the rubble. I'd look down into the dirt and the sandy pebbles would rearrange themselves like runes. One morning, there'd be a classmate's face, and it would turn out that he wasn't in school that day. Or I'd see a thundercloud, and later it would rain. I might have got the order wrong, but it sounds better that way.

It was no effort at all to see these things. The clues to everything were there if you knew how to look. Mum had her eyes open but she never seemed to see. Instead, she watched the cars, other people, her watch. My older sister used to see, but she looked at different things as years went on, too.

One morning, the sky was dull as a puddle, leaking. The fields seemed tamed. Flattened. The world shone grey. The stones looked to me that morning like wounds. I passed the stone ridge which jutted out past the closed gate of the big house. In summer, when the grass was thick and the stones were dry, I'd jump off the top ledge. I'd stand for a moment, feeling my body wobble with the height, then drop into a roll. You had to wait until the wind was right, until your balance was perfect, or you'd land wrong and bruise a rib or fall the other way, back into the nettles.

The big house was casting shadows over the ledge that day – pockets of dark dancing across its surface. When I blinked I saw myself standing on it, waving. As if I was waving goodbye. What did it mean? I looked down into the stones for answers, but Mum's voice pulled me out of my daydream.

"Would you look where you're going?" She tugged at my coat sleeve, narrowly pulling me out of the way of someone coming down the path. I felt as though I'd been jerked out of sleep. Mum rarely raised her voice, and tears pricked at my eyelids at the shame of it. I apologised and dragged my feet, tripping myself up.

The scaly, elephant-skin of my knees resisted but

the sharp stones needled their way in, beads of blood forming, dripping. My tears came just as fast. Mum dabbed the cut with a tissue. Said with a sigh, it's ok, it's not that deep, we still need to get you to school. Sorry, I shouldn't have shouted. But I couldn't stop looking at my knee. The blood ran in rivulets down my shinbone.

That night, Mum sat me on a high stool in the kitchen. The school nurse had put a plaster on my knee and she took it off, dabbed the cut with TCP, put another plaster back on. The steely tang of the disinfectant hung in the air and Jerry Springer was on TV. That was the first time that I realised – really realised – that Dad was gone. And that Mum was not the same. Perhaps nothing was.

The next morning, walking to school, there were no shapes in the stones. Maybe they'd disappeared, or perhaps I'd just stopped looking. Either way, there was nothing to see but gaping hollows that had once been full.

The Tumble-Down Wall

I'm not sure why we always sat there. It was hard and uncomfortable and prone to giving way – there were much better places to sit and drink flat beer. But this particular spot was far out enough in the fields - half way between South Anston and Todwick – that no one from the village would be able to stop and ask us what we were doing. The sky was so open out there, unashamedly colourful, resplendent at any time of day. The summer I turned 14, I stopped writing books in my room and started wandering out there to do not very much. Every teenager is angry, and so was I.

The bright yellow rapeseed fought its way into

our nostrils, and birds carved through the clouds overhead in their inexplicable formations. There was a flat expanse of dirt where the boys could take the skateboards, practise their flips and ollies, while we girls sat and watched.

"What's Wales like, then?" Jon asked me. He had a belt on with metal studs that did nothing to keep up his low-slung jeans. He had a hostile way of asking me these things, as if moving away was something I'd decided to do.

"I don't know, do I? Haven't been since I was a baby. But Auntie Jane's moved there and mum thinks it'll be... easier."

He kicked at the dirt. "You're not even going to understand what they're saying."

"I know," I took a swig of my beer. "Don't fucking remind me." I loved swearing. The words felt spiky on my tongue and I liked to watch people's reactions. Swearing made me feel like I had some impact on a world that was spinning so quickly out of my control.

We always stayed out late. Truthfully, we barely felt the cold – there was always adrenaline rushing through our veins for one reason or another. Jon gave me his jumper –a khaki Quicksilver hoodie that was about three sizes too big for me.

"Keep it. In case it gets cold in Wales," he said as we shuffled our way back to the village.

The Road

The time to go came too soon. Mum had rented a white van and the back was packed full of our stuff, leaving the house a bare skeleton. The front part had three seats and I sat in the middle, between mum and my sister. I had a duvet on my lap, all balled up in my fists. My sister said it was because there was no room in the back for it, but I suspected she needed the comfort just as much as me.

The van had tiny windows so I could only see behind us in the wing mirror. Jon and the others were there to see us off. The mirror distorted their bodies so that they seemed twisted, unfamiliar. They were laughing and yelling and I envied them so much that I felt it as a physical pain – I envied the fact that tonight, they'd go home to their beds in the same town they'd always known. I'd spend months shedding my skin, resenting my accent like it was a snake in my mouth, but I didn't know any of that yet.

We set off with a sad lurch. The roads in our village were quiet until you got to the roundabout at the bottom of the hill. It was then that my sister looked up into the rear-view mirror and told me the others were following behind on their boards. *Californication* by the Red Hot Chili Peppers was playing and I cried until we got to Birmingham. Even now, when I hear that song it's accompanied by the skittering roll of skateboard wheels.

The Map

I've never been back there - not in 14 years. Half of my life. I used to think that place was the centre of the universe but I know that it was just a village twenty minutes' outside of Sheffield, quiet and anonymous. Just like hundreds, if not thousands, more throughout the country. It is not special or unusual. I am not special or unusual. But to know me is to know the unspoken map behind my eyes.

I have no photos of it. We have pictures from inside the house – birthday parties, twinkling

Christmas trees, first days of school – but of the actual town, I have nothing.

My sister went back a few years ago. She told me how small it seemed; the streets like rows of gingerbread houses, the gardens tiny squares of emerald, proudly kept. She said it looked like toy town.

Although it's less than an hour away from where I live now, I can't bring myself to go. But sometimes, if I can't sleep, I take myself walking there. I trace the worn old lines of that map. I start by the pond in the garden, and then follow the fields to the stone ledge on the old dirt road. As the sun sets I'll sit on the tumble-down wall a while. But then it's time to leave.

It's always time to leave.

The Great Jigsaw Cat-astrophe
Christina O'Reilly

Just finishing my puzzle, just a few pieces to go
When there's a massive thud and a blur of fuzz. "Oh no!"
It's Jessie cat, she's running through the room at a frantic pace,
She landing on the table, skidding all over the place.
It's sticking to her tummy, paw and tail,
Flying through the air at a whirling dervish rate,
Pinging and ponging all over the place.
"The puzzle," I cry as she heading to the hall
Crossing to the lounge, I'm shouting, "Closes the doors."
I hear laughter coming from the room
They realise it not funny when they see my face.
She makes a dash for the door but luckily it's in place.
Jessie's picked up and she's cuddled, purring away.
While I go round and try to find the pieces everywhere.
Hoping that I've found them, I sink down in my chair.
With a sigh I start again.

When hands come over my shoulder, dropping
pieces in front of me,
Seats are being pulled out. I've lots of company,
Everyone is helping, it's turning into fun,
When suddenly the calm is broken by a thud.
We turn towards the door
There's that Jessie cat scampering across the floor.

The Dimples in Her Cheeks
Andrew Milne

I noticed her cast her gaze from a distance. I held mine for a second and then looked away when awkwardness was about to rear its head. She was sitting at a little table outside a coffee shop at the train station. There were two women, noticeably older, sitting with her. I decided they were her Mother and Aunt. Relieved that it wasn't a bloke, I could carry on my story. I glanced down at my phone, pretending to look busy. I wasn't. I swung a quick glance in her direction, our eyes met again. *Something's going on here, it must be.* If she was that enthralled in conversation, she wouldn't have looked over again. I shot my head back to my phone. I couldn't appear too interested, a second to far could have tipped me into the creep category.

Fixated, I found it harder and harder to look away. It was as if everything else around me had dissolved out of sight and it was just me and her in this world. Her mocha brown hair fell to shoulder length, it wasn't straightened, she let it fall where it may. I had to squint, but she appeared to be wearing little to no makeup. The dimples in her cheeks, the…

'Hey, would you mind taking a quick photo of us?'

I snapped out of my telescopic gaze and looked up, a tallish guy with a *Grade A* beard was looking down at me holding out a camera.

Who the fuck has their picture taken in a train station?

I had no choice but to oblige. I could think of no good reason why I should refuse. The guy looked like he was already set for the photo, bearing an elongated smile. His wife/partner/lover/mistress was standing a few steps back, also smiling, but it was a closed mouth smile. She was saving hers for the real deal.

'Of course.'

I answered with such forced enthusiasm, he probably thought I enjoyed doing this sort of shit with my time. I snagged a quick glance over at the woman with the dimples in her cheeks, not wanting to appear rude, or that I may have forgotten her. She appeared deep in conversation. What if she thinks I have ignored her?

'Thank you so much. If you could just take it over there by the sign that would be great'.

THE SIGN! This would mean I would have to get up, walk ten paces, and wait for thirty seconds while they twiddled around and got into position. *And I!* I would run the terrible risk of losing my bench I had been so fortunate to obtain. All because this lanky motherfucker and his overly white teeth wants to appear like he's got a great life on the internet. Well fuck you Mr! Get on a bench and get in the real world!

'Sure, no problem.'

I practically snatched the camera out of his hand and ushered them over to the sign, as if a concert had just finished, and we were all bustling to get out but didn't want to resort to physically shoving each other.

As we walked over to the station sign, I tried to see if she was still there out of my peripherals. It appeared she was, and she was still talking. Maybe she had seen my conundrum and thought it a great noble act that I was doing. As I continued walking, I took a moment to take a quick pan of the station, it appeared as though there was more desire to take pictures in a station than I had immediately presumed. There were groups of friends, families, more couples, and an elderly man with what appeared to be one of those long sticks which you can attach to your phone. There were a whole train of family members from differing generations, gleaming in a line behind him.

She was still there, and we'd arrived at the sign. A feeling of anxiety began to creep up inside of me. As the couple positioned themselves by the sign, I realised I would have to turn my back on the girl with the dimples in her cheeks, who at this point I'd practically planned our first weekend away together. There would be no such photo taking or stretched out sticks with phones on our holiday. We would indulge in walks around a glistening clear blue lake, encircled by pines and bustling wildlife. *Pure beauty*.

As I snapped my mind back to the current task, it appeared that I may have indulged in my romantic break for too long. The couple were there all positioned and ready to go, as if their cheeks would crack if they continued to smile a moment longer. I think the guy had probably been smiling this whole time. No sooner had the camera lens reached my eye, I snapped the photo and whipped my arm out to return the camera. There was no time for,

 Did that turn out ok?

Or, *would you like me to take another one*?

I spun around. Time in my head was passing incredibly slowly. I almost didn't want to look over in her direction for the fear of her not being there, another lost opportunity, the lake, her cheeks. It was all too much. Through the gaps in the commuters passing by, I could just about make her out. I turned 45 degrees, forgetting about the bench. T.I.M.E. P.A.S.S.I.N.G. S.L.O.W.

It was still empty. I practically charged at it, sat down, and settled in. Shimmying about slightly to get into the same position. I looked over, feeling excited. There she was. Those perfect dimples diving deeper into her cheeks every time she expressed a smile. Her long green trench coat and brown coloured jumper. Oozing style.

And then.

She looked over and caught my eye. I could see it all so clearly now. A stately home overlooking the glistening lake. Built at the turn of the twentieth century, each brick of its four storeys had earned their rightful place in time. I looked away.

When I looked back a moment later, my view was obscured by two middle-aged men staring up at the tiny information board. Their position fixated in time.

There're only four fucking platforms!

The platforms aren't going to change their location by the time you've arrived there. I couldn't make her out at all now. Why did I look away so quickly before? Maybe that was my chance? The two men continued their gaze at the screen. One of them reached into his pocket, pulled out his phone and held it up in the direction of the screen.

Seriously, c'mon.

'Excuse me, would you mind taking a photo of the both…'

I shot my head around quicker than before, meeting my eyes on two teenage girls holding out their phone.

What the fuck is…

I looked back. The blockage caused by the middle-aged men had now been removed.

And so had she.

The seats once filled with hope, promise, and opportunity. Snatched away. Gone.

I guess I can just carry on doing a whole lot of nothing now.

The New Normal
Leanne Cairns

July 29th 1994

What was that noise?
Mum and Dad are shouting.
It's 11:30pm
If I can hear them this loud, next door MUST be able to hear them.

July 30th

What am I going to do – they are arguing again
Is it my fault ? – have I done something wrong?
Oh no, that's the door.
Slam.
Oh god. Who's gone?
I dare not go out of my room.
Why me?
My friends' mums and dads are all so happy.
Why can't mine be?
I wish my life was different.
Simpler, maybe.
Bang, crash. I'm guessing dad left. I should go comfort Mum but I don't think I can.

July 31st

And again they think I don't hear but I do.
Mum and dad are supposed to guide me, not implode themselves. I can't agree with either because I mustn't pick sides.
I love them both.

August 1st

Mum asked me the other day how much of their conversations I had heard. I shrugged it off with the normal teenage response of 'not much'.

She didn't buy it. I was going to ask whether I had caused the tension, but I am too scared to.

August 2nd

Dad's turn.

Why can't parents, even warring ones, communicate?

It would make my life so much easier.

He asked me if I was ok (with the help of fast food).

Something is definitely going to happen.

Families should come with a warning. I am going to be a statistic.

August 10th 1994

Sorry I haven't written for a while. I can't believe It's happened. He's gone.

He was gone by the time we had gotten back from the hairdressers'. That's it, my life's over.

No more happy families.

Mum in pieces, I'm trying to pull her through. Nan and grandad are helping but they live so far away.

August 11th

Well he came to collect the last of his stuff. Mum only gave him one shoe of a pair and drowned all his suits in aftershave.

It has only just dawned on me that someone else's family could be hurting this way too.

I will try and broach it with him to try and find out if there is someone else.

August 15th

Well, I asked him. It's her. Why does it have to be her? She's done it before, I know.

I'm confused.

She's a lot older than my mum.

She's so wrong for him. He's my dad. He doesn't feel guilty, I know.

I was so close to her youngest daughter. Now we are lost.

It's weird I still see Mum battling whether to set him a place at dinner and just at the last moment remembering. It's heartbreaking, and I don't know how to help her.

16th August

He came over today. He's staying with his dad in Leeds. He asked mum for the answer phone and during the furore the phone ended up on the stones from my mother's discus-like throw. Mum started to shake through stress and worry.

5th September 1994

Back at school. It's strange. Mr Whitwell had us in school to see how we are coping after he left. Mum works in the school so she has the school support. Felt sick this morning but I knew I had to get on with it. Mum needs me. I need to be strong. Oh, forgot to say at the end of the holidays he hid. Saw us at the train station and HID.

October 10th 1994

My brother's birthday is in a week and I am worried about him. He has had to become the man of the house. A lot for him to handle.
He will be 10.
Not a man.
It will be different, and very stressful.

November 7th 1994

It is starting to get easier. Still can't believe he did it but it is getting better. Next month it's a first. Christmas. The first one with just us three.
I think my nan and grandad are staying so it should be ok. But you never know.

December 10

4 months since the worst day of my life.
Christmas is getting nearer. I think the day itself will be very very different but we are now strong and can do it.

December 25 1994

The day. The day I've been dreading. Christmas time to start anew. Still hear mum sobbing but she's getting better. The new normal begins today. It's time to get on with things. Most people start at New Year.
We start now.

August 10 1995

It's a year now since he said goodbye. Mum seems better. She's stopped setting him places at the dinner table. We plan to go on a family holiday in two weeks with nan and grandad.

Life has got better. Better than I thought, anyway.
My brother is slowly relaxing, thank god.
Welcome to the new normal.

Jaws – the New Era

Patrick Lawn

The top managing doctor in charge of the main hospital in a holiday resort in Florida is named Dr Richard Hahabb. He is out for a stroll along the pier and sea front one afternoon and decides to put some coins into the harbour public telescope. He moves the telescope around until his desired view of the packed and crowded beach is in sight. He focuses on all of the people and families sunbathing on the beach and lying on airbeds and sitting on deckchairs. He sees children paddling in inflatable dinghies and parents and children throwing Frisbees. He sees the children building sand castles in the sand and using their buckets and spades.

Out at sea recently there has been a number of shark sightings and sharks seen floating in the local holiday resort. Although the sharks have been seen floating around out at sea the local holiday makers on the beach have not been alerted or warned about the sharks as yet. This is because the lifeguard and the beach warden don't want to scare everyone off the beach because at the moment there is no immediate danger to swimmers and people on the beach.

But one day at around 3pm in the afternoon, a very large shark which is the biggest of the pack slowly and quietly moves in on the unsuspecting swimmers in the water. The shark creeps up on this young boy who is about nine years old. He is in a rubber dinghy and is not at all aware of the approaching shark. It surges into the dinghy and pushes the boy up out of the boat and into the water. The boy is screaming and waving his hands about and splashing about. The shark bites the boy on the leg and drags him under the water. The boy's leg is completely bitten off at the top of his leg above his knee cap. There is a lot of blood in the water and then the boy is bitten right across the top half of his body and is killed and completely devoured and eaten by the sharp with its razor-sharp teeth.

The other swimmers around see the incident take place and start swimming towards the beach. They are terrified and very scared. Everyone who has been in the water had managed to get out and onto the beach before any one else was attacked and eaten alive. The doctor who is in charge of the hospital is called Richard Hahabb. He's also in charge of the seaside town where the attack occurred. He orders the beach to be closed until further investigations take place and the predators are got rid of. The local businesses are not happy about this as they will lose money. This includes amusement arcades, souvenir shops, restaurants and hotels. They will lose customers but people's safety has to come first and be top priority.

Ode To A Vampire
Lynne Parkin

My dark Vampire, you inspire me to write.
How I love the way you hide, stalk and fly.
Invading my mind at dusk and through the night.
Always dreaming about the memories.

Let me measure your wonderful face.
You are so gothic, archetype and scary.
Trees cover your pale from the blazing place.
Summertime could be your obituary.

So do I really hate you? Not in all my days.
The love of those slender fingers and fangs.
Thinking of your dark eyes melt my heart always.
My love sealed in your one bite.

Now I too must stay away from light not dark.

The things you do to stay in a lover's heart.

Radio Lagos

Kev Paylor

'This is the U.S.S. Nimitz, we are going to bombard Lagos.' A voice then came over the emergency channel from the Nigerian Coastguard.

'This is Radio Lagos, will officers at anchor in the vicinity of the Lagos Delta cease abusing the radio channel. The channels are for official use only.'

This was followed by a loud raspberry from the *Nimitz*, the name given to the ship by the *American Light Entertainment Officer*. The purpose of this was to alienate the boredom of Junior Officers on anchor watches, waiting to discharge their cargos and get out of Lagos after months at anchor.

Nigeria in the late 1970s was a massive building programme with its wealth gained from oil. From wealth, came corruption, resulting in the cement quotas being creatively accounted for.

The morning's entertainment was now over, and the Junior Officer got on with his watch-keeping duties. He was on alert, as is the nature of a watch-keeping officer. He viewed the radar then scanned all around with binoculars, bored out of his skull!

This was the worse trip he had *ever* been on, remembering the first time to the German Democratic Republic. He was greeted while walking down the gangway to read draft marks, ready for loading, all while a rifle was trained on him. Not exactly a barrel of laughs. Rostock had been boring, the highlight was the Bratwurst, sold on every street corner, knowing he was being watched by the Stasi. *Cement*! Bloody stuff, a messy awkward cargo to be kept dry at all times, on red-alert at the slightest hint of rain.

Now in Lagos, four months at anchor, it reminded him of the words of Samuel Johnson:

A ship is like a prison except you can drown on a ship.

Yes, he got ashore and indeed Lagos was a vibrant, exciting place, but shore leave was infrequent. What really pissed him off today was that he and the crew had to smarten up the ship for cargo owners, coming to mix with their underlings as those pompous fat-cats believed. Indeed, a swanky do with the best food and wine the chief steward and chef could muster. Quite different to the usual night of shotcans and *Dance of the Flaming Arseholes*.

The shotcan had been invited by the Americans working on the North Sea oil rigs during the early '70s, basically to win drinking competitions with their Scot counterparts. A bet would be wagered by the Americans as to who can drink a can of beer the quickest. The Scots agreed while an American politely asked if he could insert a hole in the bottom side of the can of beer and suck for a few seconds. Indeed, the appliance of science, creating a vacuum on go! The ring pull opened and there was no air in the American's can, the beer shot out in a few seconds. Ingeniously, the Americans had taught us how to get hammered in a short space of time in between watches and then sleep it off.

Next was the *Dance of the Flaming Arseholes*. Contestants would strip naked, ram a roll of newspaper up their backside, and have it set alight while performing a dance. For health and safety reasons, a fire-bucket of water was ready to dowse twinkle-toes arse when things got too hot for him. The dance stopped when contestant's shouted, *Ginger Rogers!* They were judged by a panel of Senior Officers who gave points out of ten in three categories; star quality, artistic interpretation, and duration of the dance.

The dance was interrupted last night when the crew alerted a suspected pirate attack. The 2nd Officer, having just performed, ran onto the deck naked, his backside dripping wet and burnt newspaper stuck to his arse, demanding respect to get all hands-on-deck. Luckily, as the motor launch approached, they appeared unarmed and probably opportunists. Yet, they kept coming closer as if to intimidate. We were a totally non-armed merchant ship. The only ammunition before us was the rows of empty Carling Black Label beer bottles. The Bosun took the initiative and started hurling the bottles at the motor launch, and like a load of football hooligans, we joined in shouting obscenities. It worked. The launch sped off into the night. Yet, it had been a warning.

It was nearly time to knock off, get a quick shower, have lunch, then straight to bed. The midday sun had a haze around it, caused by the humidity, yet the delicate Westerly breeze made the overall conditions pleasant. The sea was a steely-blue, hard edge crests caused by the wind, forming crystalised tips like the stinging manes of seahorses. The water itself appeared hospitable yet had a menace to it. The treacherous currents were all consuming.

'This is the U.S.S Nimitz, we are now under the Nigerian flag and declare war on Honolulu.'

'This is Radio Lagos; we are not amused, we will be tracking down the culprit of these breaches by means of *Direction-Finding Equipment.'*

There was a silence, followed by the *Nigerian National Anthem* played at the wrong speed. Closely followed by Don Mclean's, *American Pie.* Ten out of Ten for the Yank today.

He wrote in the ships log, nothing to report and handed over to the 2nd Officer. Within an hour, he was in deep sleep, waking to the Captains voice from the cabin intercom. The guests were soon arriving and could he and the Senior Cadet meet them at the gangway. Sea-lovers, as a rule, hated these occasions. A ship was their home and the *landlubbers* came on board not respecting this issue.

He stood at the head of the gangway, feeling like a hotel bell-boy. He was a navigator, now reduced as a mannequin, complete with tropical whites and gold epaulets. The sun was setting, a black sun, foreboding as the guests arrived. The cordial greetings just a sombre nod and he led the way to the officer's bar. Soon the social gathering was lighting up. The cargo owner and his wife stood talking to the Captain while the Junior Officers stood distanced, like prostitutes at a wedding ceremony, the whole thing was contrived. The Captain was feeling as pissed off as his Junior Officers.

As midnight passed, the guests were either too tired or too drunk to eat anymore. The Junior Officer and Randy Andy escorted the guests onto their launch, this time there was more cordiality, especially from the cargo owner's wife who gave Andy a surreptitious kiss on the lips. Even the *pompous* ass of a cargo owner wished the Junior Officer goodnight.

The wake of the launch soon disappeared, and a lone feeling descended on the ship. It was a pain having guests but was a break from the routine. Now, back to being alert and the ever-menacing vulnerability of a hostile climate, made essential by a sudden squall.

A slight hangover from the night before was acceptable yet he was trained - responsive and alert.

'This is the U.S.S. Nimitz, we are to invade Lagos and set-up a new political party. The name of this party is to be called, *Bring a Bottle*.'

'This is Radio Lagos, you have had your last warning, any further abuse of the *emergency claimed* will result in imprisonment.'

Followed by the sound of Elvis Presley singing, *Jailhouse Rock.* The Yank was in good form today.

His attention then suddenly focused on a launch near the horizon, looking rather suspicious. As it got closer, the fear prompted his actions. The Junior Officer took quick bearings and identified the motor launch as the same one from the previous night. This time they were armed with assault rifles. He sounded the ship's alarm and ran on to the deck, positioning himself on top of the hatch, armed with what seemed like a rocket launcher. It was, in fact, the ship to shore pyrotechnics lifeline, taken from the side of the bridge.

The pirates got closer then screamed, 'Don't Shoot!' as the assault rifles were tossed into the water. The crew assembled on the deck, the danger had passed.

Two days later, they had got the call up to discharge the cargo in the safety of Lagos harbour. News came through of how a Dutch crew had their eyes cut out and the Captain and Officers shot dead by pirates.

It troubled him for a few days. When he did rationalise the situation, helped with a few shortcans, he remembered the quotation:

Strange things happen at sea.
It seemed to calm him.

Life is Full of Surprises
Timothy Wynn-Werninck

Sat in his local, his eye cast over the motley crew with the usual well-toned phrases. Flo had just finished her cleaning after another eighteen-hour shift. She liked the job despite being on the minimum wage. She was glad to have just enough put by to survive. She missed her husband who died twenty years back to the day.

The pub's monotony was broken up with youth who shared a bottle of Prosecco. They decided to play Monopoly and wished they had this sort of money to live the high life. They soon gave up, preferring to play *Twenty Questions* on their mobiles. The main thing was they were happy and fought the troubled times together as friends.

It was then he noticed a woman sat in the corner. He thought he knew her from somewhere. Her face was familiar. He remembered now. He went up to her and in a confident manner said, 'Hello, Anna. How are you?'

She smiled and said, 'I am very well, and sorry, I am terrible at names.'

'Jim. I remember you well, we met on the first day of school. You were my first love. I remember your pigtails.'

'You remember that?' She smiled in a beguiling way.

'Yes, do you remember that kiss? It was good for me. How about you?'

She fluttered her eyelids and fixed her eyes on him. She gave him a wink and softly said in a low deep voice,

'It did it for me too.'

'I thought it did.'

They drank and talked and drank some more into the night. Back at his Hovel, all that was left in the fridge were the left-overs of last night's curry. He didn't feel tired, he felt enlightened for a moment, but this soon passed. He became bored and decided to reflect on his *lonely* life in a *lonely* street, in a *lonely* community.

He stared at the television. The woman on the screen was famous, but there was something else. It was Anna. A vague memory of the evening was roaming in his mind. The problem was, who would believe him? It was then he had total respect for her at the embarrassment of his lustful ways.

The Morning After.

It was the *Reading Herald* that was delivered through the door. He was now front-page news. He was now besieged. The phone rang, it was the Nationals. Oh God, this is what it was to be famous. Least it did not go further, or did it? How far did it go? How much did he have to drink?

He did notice an improvement in his street cred. He got to the office early and tried to keep busy.

There was a message from the girl with pigtails.

She wanted to meet again.

My Escape
Esther Clare Griffiths

Smoke spiralled bitter sweet, sweeping away from the terraced house I knew as home. Leaving was easy, the next seven months terrified me. I stroked my belly softly, lost for a moment in fairytale ends. But I was trapped in a drizzly present. A fine coat of Irish rain wetting my eyelashes, like tears glistening in the night. Cold, cutting air stung my face. I dipped my nose under a deep grey scarf, watching Ma and Da stoop to carry bags, suddenly frail in the pale morning. I swallowed the guilt, but it caught in my throat and I coughed white clouds into the thick grey air. My fingers ivory against my small suitcase, wound tight - as though by holding fast I might be swept away. I heard Ma's voice, soft, pained, *Sure, God sees everything love, we can never run, not even round the corner*. Could God understand torment, real torment, could he see my turmoil? He had given up his only son to save humanity, while I must lose my child - for what? To quench a thirst for religious morality? To stop my baby living in mortal sin? I kicked the ground. *I just can't bear to give her up*, words like thunder in my head. Somewhere deep, I knew she was a girl, one I would love more than I dared breathe. The shame of my secret burnt fast and furious, a constant smouldering torch. But shame paled against the love I could already feel flickering, strong and sure.

I twisted the waist-tie around my fingers until they lost their blood turning a blue white. Without really seeing, I let the blood drain back, threading its way slowly, bringing a pale peach hue to each finger. The car crunched through the pebbles in the drive, white chalk stones, smooth, matt. I saw Ma, Da, my wee brother dragging cases into the porch, a surprised joy rippling through their voices. They hadn't wanted to leave, and yet they were caught up with the novelty of a new home. I turned away, my grief too stark, bitter, swirling like water at a drain. I waited, frozen to my seat. I couldn't even muster a glimmer of excitement. I was stuck with no escape from my feelings. Eventually Ma opened the car door, her eyes alight,

'Come on love. Sure, the sun is even out now and we can make a start on the house. It'll be a home in no time, so it will. Just you wait and see. Give me your hand love, I'll help you out.'

Ma's rough, white hand pulled me gently from the warm car, forcing me to stand, unsteady, unwilling. 'Come on love,' she urged again, as though coaxing a child into the water. Anger burned slow, silent, catching light, a sudden fire raging through me. I let myself be pulled inside.

I must stay inside. If anyone sees me, our family name will be in ruins. So I stagger from room to room, my belly stretching in front of me like a vast iceberg. As I stare through dusty net curtains, the world takes on a white dappled mesh of pattern. Everything edged with ivory. I try and picture winter. White net snakes into swathes of bright snowfall, it sparkles and shimmers in every cold step. I can't quite reach the ice in my mind. Heat from my baby bump and summer straining in through closed windows is so stifling I could scream. Instead I lie listless, waiting. Every tiny foot kicking brings me back to this room, fetid and still – the only fresh air when Da leaves and returns from work. My brother plays in the garden, squeals and shouts filtering, shadowy through my wall of glass. Against my better judgement, I imagine my baby. I name her Maeve. I dress her in primrose yellow, and hold her in the crook of my arm. She nestles, content. A moth to a flame, I am drawn to fantasy, my only true escape.

Da's eyes never light on me for more than a second, as though by not really seeing me, my bump might disappear. I know he won't want to talk about Maeve. Stony and silent, we swap faint smiles - until one night of anxious dreams wakes me in a surge of panic. I almost fall down the stairs in my rush to find him. Da sits head in hands, hair suddenly so thin, barely covering his head. I speak in a rush, spewing words like rain, quiet, begging.

'See when the baby comes, Da, could we keep her, even just for a while? Sure, no-one would need to know. We could stay home so we could. I could take her around the garden. Please Da, *please*. Sure, I know it sounds dramatic, but I feel like it will kill me to give her up. If we kept her, even just for a little while. Da, I promise we'd be no trouble. Please.'

Dad is ashen, crushed. I see his torment. I am still his little girl, barely an adult. His forehead crowds into a hundred worry lines, his eyes leak pain. I sense hesitation and for a brief moment hope soars, then crashes.

'No love, we just can't. Sure you know how your Ma feels about lying. She couldn't live with the guilt. Like she says, God sees everything. I'm so sorry love, it's the only way....Now let's get you back to bed. God knows, it's late.'

It is all too late. Da looks so hopeless, my heart aches with a sadness deeper than I've ever known.

When Maeve finally comes, I have my dream, she lies in my arms feeding. A light I have never seen drips from her eyes. She is worth all the hot towels and raw pain. Ma handing me rolled sheets to bite down so the birth is almost silent. My brother doesn't even stir. I can't hear Da's snores, I guess he's awake listening to stifled cries and hot water running on and on. I give in to Maeve. I know she is only temporary, but isn't everything in this life? Save love, I remind myself, save love. I let myself glide into her world. Waking every couple of hours to feed, our bodies merge. Our sleep murmurs gently, soft and ragged round the edges. We escape together. In the depths of deep sleep deprivation, I tingle with joy. Swept up with love for my wee girl. It swallows me like a wave, crescendos and falls, spilling my care like drops of sunshine. Fresh dew in the dawn.

Even my parents, care-worn, pale, cannot topple me. I am a part of Maeve and she of me. We are so strong. Surely too entwined to be separate? I lie watching her sleep and can't resist stroking her soft, soft skin. Sometimes as dusk settles, in the comfort of night, I dare dream of our future. Hand in hand chasing butterflies, laughing as jam dribbles down our chins, fetching firewood and telling stories late into the night. More like sisters than mother and *daughter*. The word catches in my throat and slowly, like a whirlwind gathering speed, I begin to feel the dread, hammering at my bedroom door, destroying all the drops of sunshine. All the sleep snuggles unravel. I try to hang on, but the dread is too strong. I wake in the night tearing my nails down the sheets till they catch and bleed. I can't feel the bloody soreness. A fear greater than me is burrowing deep. When I wake with a start, Maeve has gone, a faint warmth still in the sheets. Darkness rains, sunshine stolen clean away. I lie crushed. My heart breaks, shattering like glass, a million crystal fragments, never whole again.

Like a wafer thin chrysalis, wispy, lighter than air, I am hollow, empty, carried on the wind. Days merge, I am a diver, constantly underwater, surfacing briefly at meal times, shovelling a few mouthfuls. Just a robot needing fuel. I can't cry, I can't sleep, I can't laugh. My voice becomes a silent stranger. I barely exist. Except my heart keeps beating, my lungs keep breathing. But I am a shadow falling, involuntary, fleeting, deathly quiet. Sometimes in fitful sleep, I reach out for Maeve. With a jolt, I half wake to find my bed empty. I torture myself wondering if she misses me, if she cries long hours, desolate, alone. Does her new Mother hear her cry? Is she blind to her tiny fists clenched in anger? Maybe Maeve wants me, needs me. I long for her, with every single breath, every pore, every ounce of me. My grief is too deep. I still can't cry.

A sudden sharp light makes me breathe fast. Ma steals into my room, breathless, rustling in her sunday best. An excited school girl. She speaks softly,

'Eliza love, I've just seen your wee girl, all bows and ribbons, singing her heart out in church. Sure, next sunday come and see for yourself. Mae .. she's doing grand so she is. She's walking all tall and proud, bless her. It might help with your ....you know.....your blues to see her so well cared for. Sure it can't hurt, love. Sure it can't hurt my love.'

Ma's voice fades away. I take huge gulping breaths, greedy for air, desperate to see Maeve. It tears me up. I've missed all the crawling and wobbly balancing. Her first steps. I've missed my wee girl. Oh God I've missed her. My heart actually hurts.

I wait like a starved animal for Sunday, wishing the days away. By Friday my entire body is drenched in fear. Excitement crowds in around the edges, like a curious spectator. I wake suddenly, only three in the morning. I count the hours before Church, over and over. Two hours early, I wait by the door, my hat in hand. Long minutes crawl miserably by. My legs judder to a rhythm, *come on, come on, come on*. I hold the doorframe tight to stop myself running to Church. Finally Ma is ready, she bustles me outside. I flinch from the sun, like a creature living underground, I close my eyes. Light spots dance and weave, bright, dazzling. Early sunshine still cold, I shiver. Our apple tree, without my usual frame of dusty net curtain, stretches clear and vibrant into the sky. Dew spills from the grass and splashes like tears across my feet.
    Hidden under my hat, my feet barely touch the ground. Heart thumping, adrenalin soars like a bird of prey ready to pounce, ready to rob me again. We sit quiet, Ma is on her knees praying. I bend my head, the pew digs hard into my legs. I shuffle, crossing and recrossing my legs. Waiting, waiting. Sweat pours down my back and nestles in my breasts. My milk has finally dried up. I try and keep my head fixed forward, but soon I turn. I hear voices. A little girl all swathes of creamy white rustles right past me, gliding across the pew in front. Her Mother, weary and faded, doesn't see me. I slide further down my seat, eyes riveted on *my little girl*. I catch my breath, she looks just like the photos of me as a bairn. A sharp stabbing begins to throb. I swallow away the pain, stifling a fresh flood of grief, knotted so tight I can't breathe. I long for her, an ache so deep it feels like I'm dying.

Sure you're always so dramatic, I hear Ma's voice, soft, loving. I know it seems dramatic, but that's how it feels - a disease with no cure, a slow, wasting away to death.

But I am still alive, my heart beats, my lungs breathe, only my brain is fixed, static, nowhere to go. Adrenalin becomes a raging torrent, too loud. I cover my ears, forgetting the noise is inside me. Everything goes quiet – the calm before a storm. I clench my fists so tight, my nails score deep and stay red raw. I clench them to stop the wildness bursting out of me, to stop me shouting, 'She's mine!' Instead I invent glittering conversations to lure her away, to spend hour after hour soaking up every last moment together. Still, I never dare imagine she will be mine again. It hurts too much.

I feel a small hand touch my arm. I jump, shaken out of reveries. Maeve stands in front of me, proudly offering the church basket. I gasp, breathing her in, wanting so much to hold her. I fumble fingers and thumbs for change. My hands seize up, I can barely close them over a coin. I feel her eyes scoring into my head. I am a hundred degrees. I grab a handful of coins and throw them in, not even seeing how much I've given away. But Maeve notices, 'Excuse me Miss, did you mean to put the crown in?' Her voice dances clear, full of Irish lilting melody. My fantasies are crashing around, all power and sharp salt. I shake my head, mostly because I want to keep her near me. She rakes around the basket and smiles into my eyes as she hands back the crown. Our hands touch just for a second. I breathe, 'Thank you,' barely a whisper. Maeve smiles again. I hold my breath wanting to freeze time. I smile right back at my wee girl, and in this instant I know I am home for the very first time.

A Tale By The Sea:
A Cry-L Infinity Short Story
Junior Mark Cryle

Autumn up in the Northern Isles is dreary at best and the thought of being outside does not appeal, especially with an evening that promises snow in the chilly hours of the morning. Any average person would've called it a day by sunset, even working folk, if the weather was severe enough. Leonard, however, is not as average as you'd expect. Half a year ago from the night in progress he was granted powers beyond comprehension and a chance to protect living mythical races, from those who would inflict harm, as a hero.

As: *Cry-L Infinity.*

Scottish at birth, this middle-aged man's heroic alter-ego sports a padded, light blue sweatshirt, bearing a badge on the chest with the infinity symbol, dark blue jeans with the bottoms rolled and creased into cuffs, black walking shoes, a red cap covering his brown hair, sunglasses that serve a purpose despite their impracticality on nights, with a black waterproof jacket hanging over his right shoulder and concealing his arm entirely.

Accessories include a high-tech watch on his left wrist (never leave home without one), two Desert Eagles holstered on the belt around his waist, dual Katana swords sheathed on his back, crossed and partially concealed by the jacket. Even the shoes are more than they appear, able to adapt to any terrain through thought alone.

The powers in question that he received are, as his

mantle hinted, *infinite!* At maximum output Cry-L could reshape reality as he sees fit, but his body would disintegrate in five minutes. *Literally.*

To minimise the risk Leonard confined his right arm, thus reducing the output to twenty-five percent, hence the jacket. In civilian mode, his arm would be in a cast.

How was he granted this power? By saving the Loch Ness Monster from poachers.

As far as origin stories go, Cry-L's was pretty straightforward by comparison.

Which brings us to Leonard's current situation. He travelled to Shetland to investigate the increasing activities of a Mafia faction that had a recent 'change in management' a month ago, activities that included a new market in seal skins. The local authorities are unable to act as, while it is illegal to hunt seals, there is no evidence to support the claim. No blood, no carcasses. With research, Cry-L reached a conclusion: they're not hunting seals, technically. The victims are in fact: Selkies.

Scottish Mythology. Aquatic folk who act and appear as seals, but who can shape-shift into humans by shedding their skins and turn back by putting them back on. Clothes not included.

Over the week, Leonard utilized his time at Lerwick, the main port of Shetland, learning the layout of the area in relation to Mafia activity.
It has taken longer than anticipated, but the knowledge he gained would save time during his investigations, compared to what could've been wasted going around aimlessly in unfamiliar surroundings.

In the morning of that night, Cry-L made his way to the shore, hoping to find clues that the police may have overlooked, but his attention was caught when he spied a cloaked barefoot child. A blonde girl on guard and on edge, who wandered onto the middle of incoming traffic between a taxi and a truck, with no sign of braking in time. In a blink of an eye Cry-L ran in to the road, weaved through traffic, scooped the child with his arm and reached the other side safely, without disrupting the traffic flow. In favour of ensuring the child's wellbeing he placed his plans on hold, treating her to pastries from the local baker, an offer she accepted eagerly, indicating that she hadn't eaten for some time.

Without speaking, through choice or not he couldn't tell, the young girl convinced Cry-L to follow her until they reached an old warehouse occupied by a small group of similarly clothed people, two of whom were evidently close to her as they embraced each other in comfort upon arrival.

After introductions, Cry-L learned a few things that afternoon. The first was that the two people were the child's parents as she told them what transpired. Second was she could talk, which revealed she was timid around strangers, but chief amongst the revelations came when her parents revealed that they were the Selkies that were victimised.

From what the child's father told him, they arrived on shore to change forms and perform their Dance of Remembrance, to honour those who had lost their lives in conflict. A yearly tradition. Once they'd finished, they discovered that their skins were missing, spending the rest of that night frantically searching for them, unable to change back without their skins. With no other option, especially around distrustful humans, the Selkies were forced to hide during the day while continuing their search under the cover of night, until they found refuge at the warehouses. All of which occurred a fortnight ago, which meant they were but the latest victims of this crime. Upon hearing this, in gratitude for their trust,

Cry-L vowed to reclaim what they'd lost and prevent it from happening ever again.

With all he has learned, Cry-L located the Mafia stronghold and put his plan into action, staking out the place at night within a nearby tree, having spent the time recounting events up until that moment within his mind. His head hung in shame at the memory, thinking that he could've prevented such atrocities had he known about them, but swiftly shook his head shortly after, reminding himself that there's a difference between all-powerful and all-knowing. All that mattered now, was ending it.

The plan was straightforward: stop the shipments, round-up the Mafia, return the skins, avoid collateral damage.

The first part was taken care of half an hour before at Hay's Dock, as all he did was make Swiss cheese out of the propellers and hulls, which caused the ships to sink like rocks after he cleared out the personnel. He pondered, in hindsight, if it would've been more efficient to levitate the ships and glue the crew to the decks. *Next time,* he decided.

Twenty minutes of waiting after that, his patience bore fruit as he noticed Mafia goons emerging from the building to swap sentries. The perfect time to strike. Removing his jacket to reveal his right hand, drawing out a katana while his left withdrew his pistol, he abandoned his cover to rush and knock out the older guards by hitting the base of their necks with his sword hilt, then shot down two potted plants that landed on the new guards' heads, knocking them out.

Expecting reinforcements from the entrance, Cry-L leaped up and crashed through an upper window, landing behind the goon squad of fifty, then from a distance he swung his sword that generated a gust of wind strong enough to take them down like bowling pins. Then, to wrap up, he fired enough shots at all surrounding doors to block and trap the rest of the Mafia. To a combatant, the encounter felt like it was an adrenaline-filled hour, but in reality, it all started and ended within thirty seconds.

Cry-L felt glad that he opted to go in at fifty percent output, which using both arms allowed, for as much as he enjoyed the action, time was not his to waste.

Opting to let authorities clean up the Mafia pile-up, Cry-L went back to the docks to retrieve the skins, in order to return them to their immediate owners. Locating those that were shipped out previously would take longer, but he was confident it could be done. Having set plans into motion to lead the situation to its inevitable closure, Leonard was invited by the Selkie family to join them in their moonlight dancing, in gratitude for all he'd done for them.

Despite his fatigue and how late it was, Leonard thought to himself: "I suppose one dance wouldn't hurt."

New Hope
Julie Woods

I am a cynical bastard. I am letting you know this so that you have fair warning about what you are letting yourself in for.

I recently heard on the news on BBC Radio 4 that climate change scientists have warned that greenhouse gases are increasing and are nearing the point of no return.

What effect will this have on our behaviour? Will it stop those living in grinding poverty wanting enough to eat? Will it stop people who are just about coping wanting life to be a little easier? Will it stop the Western middle-classes wanting a better car and house? It might have a negligible effect on some of the latter, but not enough to make any discernible difference to the increase in greenhouse gases and other poisons being emitted into the environment.

At the moment there are endless reports about Brexit and the forthcoming economic catastrophe. No doubt, when that fades into the distance, there will be other all-consuming concerns about pending economic recessions. In the meantime, everyone is ignoring what is staring them in the face. It is more ridiculous than rearranging deckchairs whilst the ship sinks beneath you.

We live in the age of the psychopath, whereby ruthlessly driven individuals rise to the top. They promise us economic growth, which they deliver at enormous cost to the environment. For that, they are richly rewarded.

When it comes to it, humankind is, as a whole, an incredibly stupid parasite. It is inevitable that we will go far beyond the point of no return.

But what then? Is this the end of hope?

No, I think it may just be the beginning.

There will be huge casualties. Mass flooding, drought, poisoning of waterways and landmasses will lead to a culling of the human race, and many other species as well. But it will also lead to an evolution. An evolution of new species. But also, an evolution in human thinking. If we do manage to survive with a much reduced but highly functioning civilisation, I am hopeful that it will lead to a change in our values and behaviour.

Just like, after war, people are sick of all the death, destruction and depraved behaviour, those of us who remain after the next apocalypse will question the point of what we are doing.

The cost will be high. There will be permanent scars on the planet. It will no longer be as accommodating as it once was: life will be harder for humans. But these scars will be no more than permanent, active reminders of what happens when our self-centredness and arrogance take control. The most painful lesson hard learnt, which will make it probably the most potent one there will ever be.

Wisdom will replace technological development that leads to environmental destruction. Thoughtfulness and respect will replace vacuous consumerism. We will learn not only in our heads, but also in our hearts, that we are only a small part of the planet, not owners of it. In short, we will embrace humility and respect. We will move from the age of the psychopath to the age of the wise, where loud and charismatic are replaced by quiet and thoughtfulness. Listeners will be far more valued than shouters.

We will work together to nurture and serve the world, instead of fighting each other to exploit and own it. The only common enemy world leaders will unite us against is the enemy we are currently working so hard to create – an environment not fit for human beings.

Cliched to hell, I know, but maybe a phoenix will rise out of the flames. But it will not be an aggressive, avaricious one. That one will be replaced by something much more gentle.

Punkology
Kevin Paylor

Part 1

A clash of reason, a blast of hope. Quasi-religion for the Dire Straits. *New Wave* equanimity, burning embers from the feistiness of MC5, White Panthers, to the New Model Army of punks. From fish 'n' chips to the crown jewels co-operation. Empathy and empowerment. A new tradition of love and verve.

Part 2

(A Scientific Approach to *New Wave*)

Based on the music movement of the American and British revolution which contributed to evolution. *New Wave* is the sum of, *art*, plus *design*, plus (*drama* divided by *film*,) plus *dance* multiplied by *literature*.

The mode of operation, (Gentle) *Anarchism*. To always question and never assume. Neither execution nor executed. Certainly, a slightly wasted disaffection and an ability to be original.

(Gentle) *Anarchism* is a wild philosophy, more pre-history than history. To be in tune with sensibilities of instinct and emotion. *Socialogicalised equals intelligence* dived by *community*.

Patterns emerge in what appears as *chaos*. We can understand ourselves with inspection and inquiry. The *New Wave* approach is to *de-construct* yet keep some sense of formulation.

Politics is just part of the whole. Aesthetics, ethics, theory of knowledge and metaphysics equals *New Wave* philosophy.

Politics equals, *socialist* plus *aesthetics*. *Neo Realism,* divided by *ethics,* equals *faith* plus *theory. Science* equals, *metaphysics* plus *Zen.*

The primal tendencies are synthesised to an evolutionary pattern. A *revolution* is a starting point. A sense of direction and sustainability leads to visualisation. The concept is, (gentle) *Anarchism.*

Challenge, divided by *development,* plus *communication,* equals *liberty* divided by *empowerment.*

Creating a Ripple

Ruth Middleton

She had seen the text message first
And then, made sense of the new aftershave.
Hint of vanilla, the new jumper, unusual hues.
The crisp, ironed new shirt
Looked good with his favourite trousers.

She is an arrow
Her arms outstretched, taut,
Point skyward.
Her body tingles, knees bend,
Up and forward.

Dancing shadows
Reflect the morning sun
Bright, clear, clinical blue,

She breaks through
The shocking stillness.
Foam, bubbles,
Cascade, circles her hair.

They have been together for seven years.
Creating and discovering,
experiences, new places.
Living through ordinary days, tired evenings, raised
voices,
Chatting with other woolly jumper wearing ramblers

Over ploughman's lunch's, well deserved pints of beer.
Sharing holidays, birthdays, every-days.

At home she hasn't made a fuss,
Is reluctant to cause a scene,
She still asks about his day,
Does most of the ironing,
Makes Sunday lunch and his flask of tea.
They share the dog, eat at the table,
occupy the edges of their king size bed.

Her arms crash around her ears
With every arc of the crawl.
Faster and longer,
Faster and longer,
She stretches her arms, her legs, her thoughts.
She curls into a ball
And pushes away from the cold, mosaic tiled wall.

Blue Nothing
Christina O'Reilly
(An extract from a longer piece)

It started as the Earth was about to be destroyed by us. Mankind (nothing kind about us).

Atomic bombs about to be dropped, missiles fired, all countries armed, twitching fingers on buttons waiting for the "go, go, go". Already so much destruction to the world. Would there be anyone, anything left?

And then…

It seemed to happen all at once. First the skies changed getting darker, darker. Nothing could be seen, not even the moon. Then the winds so strong; lifting buildings, cars, lorries, trees and plants. Everything twisting and turning like feathers on a breeze up, up into the skies. Nothing seemed to be returning to the earth as if gravity had been suspended. Massive bangs. Boom, boom like sonic bombs going off.

After, there was only quiet. Everything manmade had stopped working. You name it, it'd stopped.

Next came the meteor shower all over the earth. Days and days passed. We had found a bolt hole in a cave in the outland, my husband and I. We watched the meteors and saw a strange thing. Some of the meteors hit the earth and burrowed into the ground, others floated back into the sky and hovered like humming birds, the sound of their wings hanging in the air encompassing the world. Once it was over, our world was changed. Not much of the outer layer of our planet was left.

But somehow a citadel had been built. The layout like an archery target, the centre the main city. Only the chosen are allowed to live there. Next the Inner Circle divided by a small bridge and river with shops, stalls, everything you could want and living quarters for the workers. Then the inner rim; a massive circle, the depth no one knows, so wide you can only get over it in a hovercraft. The outland is next.

We are refuges in tents. With very little else, I find the people very resilient and we work together to support each other in these dark times. The next was the outer rim, bigger than anyone could imagine. There's no way to escape. Some tried and failed, never to be seen again.

Our world has become a very hard and cruel place for those who have no way of supporting themselves. You are given a choice, go live in the outland and be provided with the basics every month by The Others. Or you starve. The Others are in charge. Nobody knows how, why or where they came from. But The Others are in control, bringing food, water and other supplies by hovercraft every month.

My husband, Arthur, knew something big was coming so over the last two years he built up a supply of anything we could need and tucked it away in our cave. Waiting, he said. We would need them if we survived.

One day in our camp a woman turned up setting up a healing practice. She was strange and aloof. There were lots of whispers about where she had come from but she did an excellent job so people accepted her. Her name was Maybelle.

Maybelle turned up out of the blue and told me I had been chosen to train alongside her and take this role over in the future. I assumed this was because she was elderly, but when we talked it was like she knew something but couldn't say.

I trained well and Maybelle seemed very happy with my progress so much so she put me forward for advance training in the citadel but this could take years so I'm not holding my breath.

Every so often The Others came and took people from the outland. You never saw them again. A few months ago they took Arthur. I tried to stop them but was knocked unconscious. When I came round a couple of hours later he'd gone. My heart is broken. Maybelle looked after me. I think my sadness is affecting her so as a treat she sent me to the Inner Circle to collect her herbs and medical supplies. The hovercraft guards are not happy. I can only say the confrontation was mind boggling to watch. If I didn't know better I'd say their bodies were undulating under their skin, their speech was a hissing noise. I had been sent away so I don't know if it was a form of hissing English as I could only hear what was carried on the wind. When I was called back and put on the hovercraft no one spoke. They did not talk or move the whole journey.

Once there I escaped and headed to the drop off point to pick up Maybelle's orders. I noticed the guards following me. I tried to slip away from them but they always found me. I did a few bits of shopping, for some of the camp. I had so much to carry I roped in the guards much to their dismay. All I said was 'Maybelle'. It worked every time. I think she is high up in the Citadel. It was hot and dry in the Inner Circle. I was hungry and thirsty, so the bread, cheese, fruit and water went down well in the shade of the wall. I did offer some to the guards but they declined. I couldn't see their faces with their helmets on but they seem surprised.

Suddenly everything changed. The noise loud like someone's claws on a giant's metal blackboard and the earth shaking. The sky changing, all the blue seemed to swell into huge tornados spinning round and round like the slide of a helter-skelter, hitting the ground spreading out. I didn't know if it was liquid or powder as it rose and fell, covering everything in its path. Suddenly out of the inner rim came two halves of a globe, like a clam closing it shell, protecting itself.

Everyone was motionless except the guards. They're dragging, pulling, pushing me. I was so dizzy. My skin felt hot and throbbing, my eyes burning. I was screaming. Then he picked me up. "How is he running so fast? No one runs like that," I thought. We made it back to the hovercraft. I was dumped in my seat and fastened in. We were already moving, mowing people down. I was still screaming. The big guard tried to take my clothes off. I hit him. Wham! He hit me back. I passed out.

When I woke I was in some kind of bodysuit. I was in my seat and I had a breathing mask on. I felt I'd been bathed. I didn't move. I was cold from shock, I guess. My face hurt. I heard a noise. The guard was back. He handed me a drink and took the mask off me, nodding at the drink. It looked ok, I sipped from the cup. It tasted good. Everyone was in the same suits. I asked, "What's happening?" but I was ignored. They just drank their drinks and so did I.

Looking out the window, everywhere was a blue moving mass of cataclysmic proportion. Would anything survive on the surface? The Citadel was in the distance, it looked like a snow globe but I couldn't see anything else. I realised the craft was in some sort of bubble protecting us. Suddenly we dipped down lower and lower into the deep dark outer rim. There were lights now and many tunnels. For some reason we turned on our side. I noticed my drink didn't spill. My eyes must have shown my disbelief. The guards laughed. I pout, I didn't like them laughing at me.

Many hovercrafts were entering and landing from different directions. I saw movement to my left. Maybelle was sitting further down from me. I tried to jump out of my seat to get to her but the guard pushed me, blocking me every time.

We have entered an enormous cavern. As we set down, I am marched off the ship. Maybelle is behind me. I could feel her. We walked over to the edge of the landing strip. A smaller craft picked us up. Down we went.

My breathing tubes were replaced, the hood was pulled up over my head. I was cold and my teeth were chattering. As we went further down, it seemed to slim down like the cone of a tornado. It also reminded me of a catacomb, rows and rows of oblong shaped holes with glass boxes which reflects a slivery light tucked inside. Many have bodies inside. Is Arthur in one? I felt shaken. I wanted to scream but no one would hear me as a helmet was attached to my suit.

Panic rising, I looked for Maybelle. She pushed past the guard, hissing. Her visor is clear. Her eyes sliver like holographic paper reflecting colours. She pulled her visor down but I've seen. She grabs me saying, "Don't worry".

I think *Really*?

"I've chosen you," she says. "You're special. You're safe. I won't let anything happen to you."

It all happened so quickly. I think I've been drugged. My legs won't work. I was carried to one of the containers in a wall. Maybelle is there.

"Everything will be OK," she said over and over again. Inside the air is being sucked out.

"Don't fight it," she said.

The sides closed like a vacuum. It was suddenly warm around my feet. I looked and the blue liquid was coming in. I tried to move but can't. I felt like I was falling. My head slipped to one side. I saw Maybelle watching. Then there's nothing, nothing, noth-ing…

Another One Bites the Dust
Timothy Wynn-Werninck

You look in horror, the sign you never thought you would see. You look again in disbelief. It was like losing your best watch or losing your favourite pair of shoes. Another part of life ruined un-sunder.

You and others have good memories of the place, soon gone along with others, not fit for purpose. The dog has lost its bark, entertainment since 1921.

The company has adapted through the years with sales of pink and yellow balloons and marketing. The shop was good with special rates for EU members and help for the disabled. The staff had a good knowledge of all genres of their favourite art.

The selling of posters and mugs, to some, would have been seen as outdated, as was selling t-shirts advertising *Jurassic Park*. I like them, thought they would never become extinct.

The shop also brought in technology, the *best* headphones, sockets and adapters for the *best* listening sounds. What a rich array of entertainment, aimed for home entertainment for the masses. Soon to be gone, a shop of shelter in times of winter, providing cover from storms of rain, snow and ice.

The final sign of doom showed how much property companies cared for the leaseholder. They now advertise it as the usual prime location with a great opportunity for any business. Very soon it will have other residents in the wide entrance, there is plenty of room for four.

This writing is a woeful tale. Thank you, Amazon. You have ruined the show.

Ireland Slips Away
Esther Clare Griffiths

The sea is choppy. Great curling waves arch and fall, mesmeric, glassy. I hold tight to the barrier, fingers white against the deep wood grain. White chalk cliffs fall away, a distant smudge at the edge of grey-blue sea. A little bag hangs snug on my shoulder. I feel for Johnson monkey, his rough fur, button eyes, cold to touch. Almost lost in the wind, I hear rustling paper - a bag of sweets I snaffled from a big box marked 'Food.' Dad's quick letters sprawling stylish across brown cardboard. Mum wrote all the other boxes, clear, florid writing - like waves sweeping over, even, curled. My tummy aches deep and sore. I long for home, my own bed where I can see the sky. 'It's only temporary darling.' Mum's voice is tight, as though her jaw is locked and can only open enough to let words whistle through her teeth. I have no idea what 'temporary' means but it sounds scary. I stare hard at the fizzing waves. An endless spray of bubbles balloon and pop almost instantly. I want to touch the thick creamy froth, swirling slow, and disappear under the foam. I want to swim back to my shore.

'Let's play spies.' A little hand tugs mine, warm, impatient. I fall into our game. We steal across the sloppy deck, backs flat, edging slow, ducking fast. Wind pummels our hair. We laugh at each other and rock our heads to make our hair more crazy wild. We slide swift, slap into a man smoking,

'Hey, watch where you're going will you?'

I look at my little brother, his eyes dance. Laughter bubbles over, I squash it down fast, heart thumping quick quick quick.

'Oh, sorry, we're sorry. We didn't mean to...'

I grab my brother's hand and run, almost skidding across the deck like cartoons. We don't stop until we reach the other side and fall onto a bench, wet with sea slop spray, giggling so hard our tummies are sore.

I am quiet, tired from laughing. Weary from fear and running. The chalk cliffs are white specks, fading fast under constant fizzing bubbles. I want to turn around and head back to the chalky shore. Tears fall and splash on my hands. Like the swell of the ocean beneath me, I am full. Pain brims and bleeds. I bite the skin around my finger, hard, ruthless. Leaning into the wind, I turn deliberately from my shore before it slips away forever. Staring down into the darkness below, my eyes glaze. The ferry cuts through glass waves, carving them in half, unflinching.

'I always feel a sadness when the Irish coast disappears.'

Dad's hand is warm, rough. His hair flies everywhere in the wind.

'Will we come back soon?'

My voice is small against the wide sea, the fierce wind. I don't want to hear the answer. He clears his throat, just like always when he's worried.

'Of course darling. We'll always come back, every school holiday if you like.'

My throat is so tight with tears, I can't speak. *It's not the same. It's not the same*, words plead in my head. I turn away.

'I want to go back, please Dad, *please*.'

I grip his hand tighter.

'We can't love. There's your mum's new job, and you'll be happier at a different school. One that doesn't shove religion down your throat all day long.'

I sob into his chest, tears soon soaking his shirt.

'But I don't care about any of that. I just want to see Anna. I want to be with her, the way we always were.'

I imagine seeing Anna at Easter and my throat closes up, I gulp air. I am suffocating. Dad squeezes my hand,

'It's alright Est, you can write and talk to Anna on the phone every day. We will be back on this ferry before you know it.'

He bites the back of his hand. A nervous habit so familiar, I stop sobbing. Dad pats me briefly on the back. Clumsy. Loving. God, I love him so much. But still I want to go back. Now. *Now.* I look back for the shore line, squinting hard in the wind. But it has vanished leaving only a mass of sleek black ocean, crashing on and on. Away from Anna. Away from home. Away. A part of me is lost in the dark night ocean forever.

Only Mum
Excerpt from a Fictional Journal
Angi

September 21ˢᵗ, Wednesday

Mum's funeral 2pm.

       Funerals. Miserable affairs at the best of times. This wasn't even close. That horrible misty rain that makes everything wet and well . . . grey didn't help. Not that many people either. Just immediate family pretty much and no flowers – *"Mum wouldn't have wanted that"*. Those words had become John's mantra over the past few days since Mum's passing. As a result the church had been as dismal as the weather.

       The after reception, tea and a sandwich or sausage roll at Sam's flat (because it was nearest the church) was even worse. Being squeezed into the tiny open plan kitchen/living area with my husband's siblings,, spouses and their offspring was a new kind of Hell, but lack of space at least gave everyone the excuse to get away as quickly as possible.

       If I'd heard the words *"It's only Mum after all. She wouldn't have wanted any fuss"* once I'd heard it so many times I wanted to scream.

       Would my own boys, both *"too busy"* to take time out of their midweek schedules to attend Gran's funeral, think that about me when my time came? Was that already how they saw me?

       Perhaps this debacle wouldn't have seemed so bad if John's dad had had a similar send-off seven years ago. Instead that had been little short of a state funeral, even down to the horse drawn hearse with a sumptuous after reception most brides would have killed for.

red boots
CF

I am in the roofspace
and on finding the pair of
subdued
red leather boots
I am forced to squat and catch breath

the laces still hold tangled knots
the left boot bears the telltale scuff
of his stumbling gait

these orthopaedic boots hold a
bold history
a noble endeavour
to help bring my supine eldest son
upright

for congenital disability
has want of a good boot

for years
like two toy fire engines

they dangled from his
thread thin legs

I see now
a head picture
his sassy smile
my locked in pride

I finger brush each eyelet
and rethread the lace
through the right boot

then
setting them upright
two by two
I yearn that hour
when it was just
the want of a good boot
that held us all together

Dear Mum
Emma McKenzie

Today I made bread
For the first time
With my son standing on a chair
Our hands kneading the dough together,
It reminded me of you Mum,
In your kitchen,
Making everything from scratch
To give us the very best
In your own way,
I wonder why I have not made bread before?
The rise and fall of the dough
The kneading of a family life
My heart tugging
The dough soft in my hands

The Send-Off
Sue Richardson

Everyone who attended Mr Davis Senior's funeral knew that Martin's wife was a trollop. He'd seen enough pitying glances to know that. Martin was an upstanding member of the community. Gilly… was not.

8:07pm the night before

The argument increased. Martin was sure everyone in the village would be able to hear them shouting.

Gilly screamed, "if you had been more of a man, I'd never have had to sleep with Alex!"

The weather for Mr Davis Senior's funeral was typical for October – dim, cloudy, the rain getting heavy. There were thunderclouds in the distance. There were only a few people at the graveyard. Martin heard the coffin being lowered gently into the ground. Though he had heard this sound many times, it was extra satisfying today.

Good riddance, he thought.

9:10pm

"Come back here, don't walk away," he'd seethed at Gilly, trying to keep his voice level. They didn't need the whole neighbourhood to hear. "You've ruined me. I turned a blind eye to your flirting at the golf club – who knows how much I've turned a blind eye to. Even our bloody wedding. Twenty-five years on and you still haven't explained what you and Jack were doing in the basement of the hotel!"

He couldn't stand still, he couldn't look at her. He faced the wall instead, trembling.

She kept sipping from that damn half pint glass of gin, eyes bloodshot. She hadn't been crying though – Martin suspected she was enjoying this. "I wouldn't have had to sleep with anyone if you weren't a poor excuse for a man. All you care about are funerals, bloody funerals. You've been locked in there for five hours sorting out that sanctimonious prat Mr Davis. If you'd spent more time with me, I wouldn't have had to sleep around! It's just a bit of fun. You're so staid and boring. No one would want to touch you."

Martin turned and shook hands with Mr Davis. The funeral was small, a small turnout, possibly because of the weather.

Shame really. Mr Davis Senior had lived a good life and deserved better. He had worked hard for the church and had been on many committees.

Gilly had, too – he'd give her that. While he'd been running the funeral business, she'd kept busy. Tennis clubs, amateur dramatics. It was only in the last ten years he'd started to figure it out. He liked to see the best in people, but her affairs became harder and harder to ignore.

Oh, she'd kept busy alright.

*

10pm

"I don't think anyone was impressed at your snogging the face off Andy who built our summer house," he spat, fists clenched white at his sides. He wasn't an angry man. But he was struggling to control it now.

"It's ok maybe flirting with the window cleaner, but when you went after Sally's husband, I knew she would put a spoke in your wheel."

"Oh, fuck you! Sex with you is crap! I tried in the beginning to show you but you're bloody staid, and sex with you is about as exciting as cleaning the oven." Gilly was staying to sway on her feet, the gin taking hold. How much had she drunk?

Martin had looked at her and tried to remember how he'd loved her. He'd thought, once, that their marriage could survive. That two people in love could figure anything out.

He no longer believed that.

"Well, I've had enough. It's over, Gilly. No more. I can't stand the pitiful stares and the sympathy. No one would be surprised if I left you."

She scoffed cruelly, hands waving around like a wild thing. "You leave me! Trust me, I don't want to spend another day here, either. Living with dead bodies everywhere? I've had enough. Listen to me – everyone is going to know it was me who left you, Martin – you frigid twat."

Martin nodded respectfully at the mourners, accepted compliments on Mr Davis Senior's large coffins. It *was* nice. He'd had it upgraded to the biggest size, strong oak– they often used them for larger folk. He explained the change of coffin and said to Brian, I've given your dad a superior coffin. I believed all the good work he has done should be rewarded. I'm certain he will continue to make sure the beliefs he had on marriage will still be carried onto the next life. It's been an absolute pleasure to do his funeral.

 Brian didn't know just how much of a pleasure it had been.

10:30pm

Swinging open the back doors, Gilly stumbled out into the garden, glass in hand. She took a huge swig of gin.

"And do you know what? I enjoyed every second with Andy."

Martin stilled. He wasn't thinking straight. "Andy?" Surely not. Surely not his brother.

Gilly wandered back into the house, unsteady on her feet. She got up close to him, too close, breath reeking of stale gin. "Now, he really knew how to please a woman."

Martin's sadness was replaced by a white-hot anger. He tried to control it, placing one hand against Gilly's flushed cheek. She flinched, surprised, but didn't pull away. He let his fingers trail down her face and to her neck. He felt her heart pounding through his hands.

"Oh, Gilly. You really shouldn't have told me that."

Martin looked down at Mr Davis Senior's coffin. He'd checked it last night, when he'd tucked Gilly's dress in around her cold body. Putting his wife's body in there with him, Martin thought, really had been the best idea. No one suspected a thing. Plus, Mr Davis Senior would understand that Gilly was a trollop of a wife and had deserved what was coming to her. He'd been a good man. Much like Martin himself.

The thud of the earth hitting the solid wood was a blissful satisfaction.

Happy Poems
Anthony Stanfield

GOOD DAY
HAPPY DAY
FIRST OF MAY

2nd SUNSHINE
The sunshine and the rain
The buttercups and the campions
Tis grand to be a champion
Glistening rain
I might be in Spain
The rustle of leaves
On the roof top eaves
Sparkling water, in the river
Come children, play
Come hither and thither
The flowers eventually wither
God's carpet of flowers
For many sunshine hours

The Group
Keith

I stand and sway
Music is kept at bay
People are right into it
Keep moving and do not sit
The rock music is moving me
It's going to be good, you see.
We have six songs, before a break
So time to rock and shake
Each song is bear on new things
Drums play, a guitar sings
Vocalist is loud and hard.
What have we? A bard?
Everybody has got into the beat,
Boys and girls are ready to meet.
When the break comes along
A glass of lager instead of a song
Water over my face cools me down
Back to the floor for more sound.
The group comes out to play
Audience gets up and do it their way.
Shouting and screaming along
You can barely hear the song
The arena is buzzing to a good time
Lyrics bounce, there is no rhyme.
What an experience is has been!
You have to be there to be seen.
It's time to think about AC/DC

We will not be P.C.
The group are on fire
It will go to the wire
Loud and rocking
The noise is shocking
Let's fetch to a close
The noise hits my toes.

Volunteering with Converge

Sophie Neal

Converge has given me the opportunity to explore my creativity and think more about my own ideas, something that I have been unable to do since my high school days. Creative writing in particular has allowed me to do this with no restraints and nothing to hold me back.

Working with Converge as a student volunteer was very much like throwing myself out of my comfort zone. One of the things I have gained is the confidence to throw myself in the deep end, and the belief in myself to knowing that I will be able to keep myself afloat. I have learnt a great deal more than I ever thought I would from the students at Converge. Week after week, I have been continually amazed by their talent and skill, much of which is demonstrated here in this book for all to see.

I will be forever grateful for the experience, confidence and skills that Converge has given me and I hope it continues to be as successful and life-changing as it already is.

The Glass Enigma
Ross

It was another busy day at Glass Enterprises, a most interesting corporation. Rebecca opted to spend her lunch break with Scott. Scott always chose something quick to eat and brought it from home so he didn't have to waste time leaving the building for lunch. Rebecca always brought her own lunch so she could eat with Scott. It was a comfortable routine.

"So," began Rebecca, a pensive look in her eyes. "Have you ever noticed that Jenny makes odd things happen?"

Scott paused before he could bite his burger. "I don't know what you mean. Weird things don't happen around Jenny any more than they do around the rest of us."

"No, I don't mean they happen around her. I think things are happening because of her."

"Now hang on a minute," Scott started, "do you really believe Jen would start that fire? Or that she would endanger that baby's life like that?"

"No! Of course she wouldn't deliberately do such things, but what if she causes things to happen unknowingly?"

"What? I'm sorry Rebecca, but that theory doesn't hold much weight. I think you should just forget about it." From Scott's tone, Rebecca could tell the conversation was over.

Rebecca would not forget about it, however.

One week had passed, and everyone at the office had been assigned their "Secret Santa". Rebecca had the fortune to draw Steve; the man had a notorious sweet tooth. Rebecca was just going to grab a file when she bumped into Jenny.

"Rebecca! I'm so glad I could catch you! I was having some trouble with my Secret Santa and I was hoping I could get your advice."

"Oh really? I don't know how good I'll be with that. I'm not really good with that sort of thing. I happened to get really lucky with mine though."

"Well you and Scott are such good friends that I thought you would be the perfect person to ask."

"So Scott is yours eh? Well in that case I think you should get him-," Rebecca paused. She had been looking for a way to test her theory about Jenny for a while now and it looked like this just might be the moment she had been waiting for. "Actually, can I get back to you on that? There is something I need to check before I can be sure of what you should get him." Rebecca hoped that Jenny hadn't grown suspicious. "I'll call you, okay?"

"Sure, thanks! I have to go now, Mr Glass wants these papers sorted out in the next twenty minutes, so I have to get back to it. Bye." Jenny gave a quick wave before hurrying off. Rebecca made a note to call Scott after work.

Rebecca had just gotten home from work and was trying to recall if there was anything else she should do before she got changed. *Yes, that's right. My little project.* She dialled Scott and waited for an answer.

"Hi Rebecca. What is it? Can you either call back or make it quick, my show is going to start in five minutes and I can't record it."

"Don't worry, this will be quick," claimed Rebecca, having only just remembered that Scott's favourite crime drama started around now. "Is your kettle broken?"

"Huh? What on earth is this about? Why would you ask that?"

"Sorry, I can't explain right now, I just need to know if your kettle is broken."

"No, my kettle is working fine," Scott replied, still bewildered.

"And did you use it in the past couple of days?"

"Yes Rebecca, I used it this morning."

"All I needed to hear. Thanks. I'll let you get to your programme now, bye," said Rebecca, hanging up without another word. *And now to put this plan into motion.* Rebecca quickly dialled Jenny's number. The phone rang five times before anyone picked up, Jenny was never good with phones.

"… Hello?" came a tentative voice through the speaker.

"Hey Jen, it's me, Rebecca. You wanted me to advise you on what to get Scott, remember?"

"Oh, that's right! You got back to me quick! Please tell me."

Rebecca steeled herself. There was no undoing this and it wasn't like this would cause much harm. "Well, I just talked to Scott and confirmed something. Luckily for you, Scott's kettle broke a couple of days ago and he has not been able to scrounge up enough money for a replacement, so you should definitely get him a kettle."

"Oh, okay. Thanks. Bye," said Jenny. Soon afterwards, a dial tone could be heard.

"And now I wait," Rebecca told herself.

Several weeks had passed and everyone had received their Secret Santa gifts. Steve had very much enjoyed Rebecca's box of luxury chocolates. Funnily enough, Steve had Rebecca as *his* Secret Santa and had given her… a box of luxury chocolates. Oh well, she could always share some of them with Scott. Speaking of Scott, he was talking with Jenny right now. Rebecca decided to listen in.

"So Jenny," Scott started, "I have you to thank for my new kettle. How *did* you know?"

"Oh, I just got lucky I guess," Jen answered. Rebecca was relieved that Jenny didn't drop her name into the explanation or else things might have gotten awkward for Rebecca. "It's not like it would have gone to waste - as even if yours was fine you could always keep it as a spare. Hey, I got lucky with the present I received too. How my Secret Santa knew that I wanted a figurine of a giant dragonfly, I'll never know. Well it's-," Jenny's eye happened to glance at her watch, "-that late? Crap. I have to get going before the hardware store closes and get some more glue. Excuse me." Jenny sped off with one last wave at Scott before heading around the corner.

Scott caught Rebecca's eye and hailed her over. Perfect, this would enable her to find out the results of her little experiment.

"Hey Scott. How are you?"

"I'm doing great thanks," replied Scott. So far so good. "How are you?"

"I'm doing well. So, Scott," Rebecca started, "I overheard you talking with Jenny. It was nice of you to pretend that your kettle broke."

"Actually, I wasn't lying," he said. "My kettle broke a while back and I wasn't sure where I should get a replacement. In fact," Scott started to get a suspicious look in his eyes, "it happened shortly after you called me that time asking me if my kettle was broken. While it is nice to get a replacement, I liked my old one. Is there anything you would like to tell me, Rebecca?"

Crap. I'm in trouble, she thought.

At least she had gotten some confirmation on her theory.

All the Dead Were Strangers
Iain Barclay

David fell to his knees. The feeling of the ground beneath reassured him.

He spread his hands further apart for better balance and took some deep breaths.

Something was still not right. He had the urge to open his eyes. Why? David had been blind for more than two decades. A cold finger pricked the back of his neck and slowly dragged itself down his spine.

Lights began to dance beneath his lids. The colours and intensity changing as he moved his head.

Suddenly the world exploded! The thunderous sound of trees snapping and the ground itself reverberating from an impact.

He was lifted into the air and flipped onto his back. He hit the ground and as the breath was forced from his body, he became aware of the bright yellow light seeming to come from beyond his still closed eyes.

With the light came a fear which sat in his chest like a huge stone.

He had no idea where he was, and he suspected his blindness of more than twenty years had deserted him.

David had no recollection of the day he lost his sight. He only knew that it was protecting him from something far worse than the prospect of being blind.

Something else was stirring at the edges of his memory. Something trying to be heard.

'No!'

David flipped himself over at the sound of his own voice, like a puppy jumping at the sound of its first bark. He had to be quiet. Why though?

On his hands and knees, head facing the grass, David began the meditations he practiced if he found himself disorientated. He slowed his breathing and counted the breaths in and out. In for seven, and out for seven. In for seven, and out for seven. Better. Now listen and feel.

He lifted his face to find the sun, turning around until the warmth was strongest. This time though the brightness behind his eyes confirmed the direction. Panic flickered, but he controlled his breathing again and settled back to gather more information.

Grass below he could feel with his hands. The breeze he could feel and hear coming from his left. There were trees all around judging by the sound of branches and leaves rustling. Some bird song he didn't recognise. No traffic or people noise.

So, it was around midday, he was in a forest or woods and he was alone at least two miles from a main road.

Was he alone? That feeling came back. He was being watched. Someone staying just out of reach, taunting his blindness, biding its time, just waiting for the right moment to… to what? Jump on him? Kill him? Why?

His support workers called it blind paranoia. Almost all blind people left alone feel a presence from time to time, especially if they are in a new, stressful situation.

He would have to open his eyes and find out what was happening. Nothing made sense at the moment. He knew he was in a forest or woods but could not explain how he got there from his back garden. If he was to find a rational explanation then he would need to take a look at the world.

Shapes and shadows resolved into the bones of his hands. The light of the sun so strong it was like looking at an X-ray.

Looking down, David opened his eyes. Shades of green gradually resolved into grass.

Fear, excitement, and more fear. Why was he afraid? That awful crashing and shaking had stopped. No. The fear came from a memory buried so deep he could not even find the edges of it. His mind scampered away from the thoughts. That was why he went blind in the first place. So he would never have to witness a horror like that again. What horror? Again, his mind skittered around his skull trying to avoid the memories struggling to surface.

Well whatever was waiting for him now, he doubted it could be any worse than what was waiting for him inside his own head. He braced himself and opened his eyes.

Again the grass swam into focus. He tilted his head up and recognised the trees although not the species. Suddenly he felt someone watching him. He turned around slowly.

David's already overloaded mind gave up. Now he was seeing things that could not be.

He flopped to the ground in front of what could at first glance be mistaken for a formation of very colourful rocks. But on closer inspection turned out to be a dragon.

Tarl looked down at the sleeping form and sighed. This was not going well and he was running out of time.

This could not wait. Tarl reached down and plucked the unconscious man from the ground and leapt into the air.

The first flap of the gigantic wings flattened the grass and bent back the closest of the trees.

Still unconscious, David was hurled back to that day twenty years in the past.

The sun shone on his young face a pleasant

counterpoint to the cool breeze.

He looked out across the cornfields bordered by dense blackthorn.

As he gazed at the hedges they seemed to stir with a life of their own.

David sat forward rubbing his eyes as dark figures began to emerge from the boundaries.

Now the corn was gone. Replaced by a crowd of people held captive, their feet buried by the earth.

As the mass of humanity sensed the danger from the dark forms emerging from the hedges, their struggles became more and more frantic.

As the first of the shadows reached the outer rows of corn people, they solidified into scale clad, monsters bearing scythes in their clawed hands.

The struggles of the writhing masses grew as the first of the hedge demons reached them. Trapped by the perfidious earth they began to fall to the pitiless scythes.

Above even the sounds of the screaming was the metallic swish of the blades as they fell again and again. Slicing through flesh and bone leaving red mist in their wake of a pitiless rain of death.

The screaming began to fade as the number left able to scream diminished to a few last desperate vestiges of life, melting back to the soil that had held them captive.

The shadow demons turned and drifted back to the boundary hedges and disappeared.

David gaped at what was left. The fields lay before him like a vast butcher's waste bin after a busy Saturday afternoon.

His parents found him just before sunset, sitting beneath the tree with his hands covering his eyes and screaming.

Tarl was within sight of the city and had sent his thoughts ahead so the council could be gathered.

He had also let them know a healer would be needed.

The Twenty Thousand Pound Question

William Davidson

Jake waited for the twenty thousand pound question. He'd never thought he'd get this far.

'Are you ready?' asked the presenter.

Jake was distracted by a piece of gold ribbon on the podium in front of him. They sprinkled short strips of gold ribbons from the ceiling of the studio when someone won the jackpot. This must have been a stray piece.

'Yes, I'm ready,' said Jake.

A low drumroll echoed around him.

'What is the highest mountain…' The presenter paused.

Great, Jake thought. In England, Scarfell Pike.

'…in Africa?' said the presenter.

It wasn't Scarfell Pike. He couldn't think of any other mountain. He touched the ribbon. But it wasn't just a piece of gold ribbon. It had a word on it, and the word was *Kilimanjaro*. That was the highest mountain in Africa. He did know.

'When you're ready,' said the presenter.

This wasn't right. This was cheating. But then again, it was twenty thousand pounds. Now wasn't the time to be moral. Maybe he could say *Kilimanjaro* and destroy the evidence by discreetly eating it.

'I must press you for an answer, Jake,' she said. The drumroll stopped and the spotlight on him brightened. He felt as if he was there at the podium and also watching himself from the audience or from his sofa. He held up the ribbon.

'This ribbon says *Kilimanjaro*,' he said, 'which I didn't remember when you asked me. I can't cheat.'

The drumroll seemed to start again. But it wasn't a drumroll. It was applause.

'That's very honest,' said the presenter.

She held a finger to her earpiece.

'Honesty worthy of reward,' she said, and all the gold ribbons fell from the ceiling, and Jake threw *Kilimanjaro* up in the air.

Anyone For Coffee?

John Manby

Andrew was going for coffee today, so he was getting suited and booted. It was going to be a very exciting day. He even had the correct amount of change for his espresso.(Andrew thought Minny the waitress liked it if he had the correct change).

Andrew got to the cafe and sat at his usual place feeling a little less stressed. He had a good view of the surroundings and Minny. He was besotted with Minny, the way she walked and talked ,and the way she flicked her shoulder length hair back.

Minny came over to where Andrew was sat. "Can I take your order, Andrew"?

Well, because Minny had used Andrew's first name, this sent him all bashful and slightly weak at the knees. It was a good job he was sat down, so he could stay in control. But how was he going to react? Bold? Positive? No, instead he spluttered "Y-y-yes," espresso please in an anxious voice. As soon as Andrew had replied he thought, 'ohh heck that's blown it'; he wanted to make a good impression. He's not coming over very macho.

Minny was hard working, saving for her first car. She didn't really like her job waitressing, but once she had enough money saved to buy a car, she would leave. Today, Wednesday, wasn't one of her favourite days of the week. That Andrew would be in, no doubt.

Minny didn't like the way Andrew looked at her, and she knew from talking to her colleagues that he had the hots for her. Not that it stopped her flirting with him anyway. He was dressed up; Minny wondered if there was any mischief she could get up to.

Minny had given a little chuckle, after the way Andrew had asked for a coffee, and had visions of accidentally on purpose pouring coffee on Andrew. Her way of thinking that serving dorks wasn't in her resume.

Andrea was the manager of the café. Wednesdays were one of the quiet days, and Andrea liked running a good clean orderly café. She was a seasoned proffesional. Well even Andrea had noticed how Andrew ogled Minny, and knew things like this usually end up in disaster. Today she had noticed that Andrew was dressed rather smart, and wondered whether he had a job interview or something similar. So when Minny had chuckled at Andrew, Andrea thought she would have to have a word with her. Andrea knew Minny was gay, and that Minny didn't like Andrew too much. Even though Andrea was good at her job she was going to be amazed at what events were about to happen.

Minny was carrying a tray with Andrew's espresso. Unbeknown to her and everyone else, one of her shoe laces were undone. Then, all of a sudden she tripped, and Andrew's espresso went tumbling through the air. Just as the café door was opening, SPLOSH, all over Marcos the manager. Quicker than a flash, Andrea ran over to where Marcos was stood, but, underequipped, she only had a serviette in her hand, and like a scene out of a *Carry On* film she started to dab Marcos' trousers round the crotch area.

Meanwhile, Andrew had started laughing, a deep belly laugh at that. Because of this, Marcos swept Andrea aside and angrily boomed at Andrew, "WHAT THE HELL ARE YOU LAUGHING AT?"

Andrew couldn't stop laughing; Andrea was

rooted to the spot with an empty cup in her hand; Marcos was incensed, being soaked in coffee and with some customer laughing. He strode over to the coffee machine behind the counter, and began pouring a coffee. Then he walked calmly over to where Andrew was sat, and slowly started to dribble the contents of the cup into Andrew's lap. Instantly, Andrew stopped laughing, and his face turned bright red. He yelled out loud too. Minny this time sprang to Andrew`s aid, but what could be done? Andrew jumped up, and Minny must have thought that Andrew was in pain, because she started delicately trying to unbutton Andrews trousers; she succeeded - then Andrew's trousers slid down to his ankles.

Minny was trying to dry Andrew`s crotch with a small tea towel. Her eyes widened: she was quite amazed at the size of the bulge in Andrew`s jockeys. But the bulge wasn't Andrew. It was, in fact, a pair of socks that he'd pushed down there, to make him appear to be a lot bigger than he actually was.

But, not to put a finer point on it, that is another tale….

Books of White Water
Helen Kenwright

Berta walked into the Wellness Centre to find herself faced with a pile of crates teetering in the middle of the entrance lobby. For a moment she thought it might be one of Marta's sculptures, but if so it was considerably more orderly than usual. She meandered towards it to read the neatly-lettered labels on the side of each box. Books: H to L. Books: M to R. Books...

Books.

"Morning, Berta." Lottie strode across the lobby. She was a small woman with a very large rucksack, giving her the appearance of a long-haired turtle. "Well, well. What have we here?"

"Good morning, Lottie. No idea."

Lottie surveyed the tower. "Looks like books."

"Must be for the library, then."

"The library?"

"That's where books are usually kept."

"Well, yes, in the big cities maybe. But we don't have a library. Not the sort with books."

"I expect they're on their way to Leeds."

"But they must have come from somewhere, even if they have yet to reach their destination."

Lottie was tenacious. It made her very good at computer coding and complicated knitting, but could also make for long conversations full of conjecture, of which Berta was not fond.

"I wonder who they belong to," Lottie said.

"I dare say if that's any of our business we'll be informed. Well, can't stand here all day. Good morning."

Berta bustled off quickly to her booth, before Lottie could prolong things any further. Not only did

Berta wish to avoid hanging about in the drafty lobby all day, but a pile of books was none of her business.

Hetty was one of the main relationship and life advisors in the Wellbeing Centre, and facilitator for all the booths in what was known as the Crescent: a sweeping arc of wellbeing practitioners, each offering different skills and services to the community of White Water. Berta was officially titled a Wisdom Developer, which she detested, so everyone simply called her Berta.

Once a month, Hetty conducted what she called a 'share, don't despair' meeting for the advisors and therapists, where they were invited to support and mentor each other. Or, as Berta had put it to her apprentice, Andrea, a painful two hours where everyone talked about their work rather than doing it. Berta's gifts led to a different sort of confidentiality with her clients. Seeing into someone's heart and learning their secrets was a uniquely intimate experience. To share what she learned through her work would be more like gossip than 'raising awareness of support needs', as Hetty called it. This was the first time she'd brought Andrea along with her to one of the meetings. Berta thought it was probably about time, and Andrea, with all the enthusiasm of the uninitiated, was shockingly keen.

Hetty welcomed them with the broad smile and expansive gestures of a professional welcomer, and invited them to help themselves to refreshments. Berta chose a slice of lemon drizzle and a cup of plain mint tea. Hetty's blending skills weren't really up to scratch, but she could make a reasonable sponge.

"Give the nettle and dandelion a miss," she murmured to Andrea.

Hetty chivvied them all along to the meeting

circle. Berta settled in to enjoy her cake, and listen.

"Welcome, everyone, hello, good afternoon," said Hetty. "So lovely to see you all here."

Everyone around the circle nodded and munched. There were seven of them, including Hetty: Berta and Andrea; Lottie, Blossom, Gwen and Mike. Harold and Ed were doing a talk at the school and the arty kids (as Berta thought of them) were finishing off the new mural in the social area.

"I was wondering," Lottie said. "Does anyone know where the books came from?"

A buzz went around the circle. Books? What books? Where? Why?

"I'd rather we kept our conversation to our usual agenda, if that's all right with everyone," said Hetty. "The books are neither here nor there."

"But they are there," said Lottie, "They're stuck right *there* in the middle of the lobby where anyone could fall over them."

"I do apologise," said Mike. "So sorry. I think they must be mine."

"Must they?" said Hetty. "Well, that's nice. Can we move on?"

"I'll move them as soon as I can." Mike dipped his head apologetically in Lottie's direction. "So sorry."

Berta disapproved of Mike. He had a lot to say about what he thought to be facts, and not a great deal about how those facts related to real life. Berta had nothing against research, so long as it was kept in its proper place. She thought Mike probably couldn't decide what to have for lunch without triangulating a theory about it.

Hetty said, "Right then."

Lottie said, "I'd love to know what sort of books they are, if it's not rude to ask?"

Mike's eyes lit up. "Oh, not at all! I secured them from a private collection. They are published sets of ancient documents. Pre-cataclysm, mid to late twentieth century."

"What sort of documents?" Andrea asked. Berta gave her a sharp look, which she ignored.

"They contain details of people who were treated for various health problems. Following the quaint customs of those times, they had whole systems dealing exclusively with what they called 'problems of the mind'. No sense of holistic medicine at all, most primitive. But their approach to science is fascinating."

"And brought the entire world within a hairsbreadth of extinction," Berta said. "Best left alone, as far as I can see."

"But the stories! You can't put a value on human experience, Berta," said Mike. "You of all people should know that."

Berta took a savage slurp of tea.

"I'm sure the material is very interesting, Mike," Hetty said, soothingly. "And do report back any useful findings to us. Meanwhile, our agenda-"

"I'd have thought you'd have had a keen interest," Mike said, still addressing Berta. "Considering your current problem."

"Do I have a problem?" asked Berta, with a dangerous edge to her voice. "I was not aware."

"The refugee," Mike said. "Cara."

Cara had joined the village a few months before. She'd escaped the great droughts of the northern American States and somehow come all the way to Yorkshire, where they'd found her hiding in the overflow caves during a flood last winter. She'd lost half of one leg to infection, and been lucky to escape with her life.

They had no idea how she'd got to White Water, because Cara refused to speak about it. In fact, she barely spoke at all, and then only to Berta or Andrea, or the children who'd found her in the cave. Berta didn't make a big thing of it. Cara could say whether she wanted a second helping of soup, or if she preferred blackcurrant to peach jam. She was a very gifted artist, and spent most of her time working on the new mural in the Wellbeing Centre. She thrived on the work.

It was true that she was an enigma, a mystery of a person: she had locked her past down so hard even Berta couldn't read her. But there was more than one way to peel a peach, and to Berta's way of thinking, Cara would speak when she was good and ready.

"There are various records of people with Cara's problem," Mike said. "They called it mutism."

"I'm sure they did," Berta muttered darkly. "They had a name for everything back in those days."

"It's a symptom of trauma."

Berta turned the full force of her glare on to Mike. To her satisfaction, he flinched. "It's a symptom of choosing not to speak, that's what it is. Cara is looking very well these days, wouldn't you say, Andrea? She's eating right, she sleeps better, she doesn't wake up screaming in the night more than once a week." She didn't take her eyes off Mike.

"She's doing great," Andrea said. "I'm sure when she's ready-"

"Yes." Berta said. "When she's ready."

"And we'll do all we can in the meanwhile," said Andrea. "All of us."

Mike pounced. "And don't you think that should include reading some historical documents so we can learn from the past?"

Hetty cleared her throat loudly. "Excuse me. Our agenda. Blossom, would you like to start us off?"

Blossom looked up suddenly from his cake, startled as a deer in a thunderstorm. "Me?"

"It's your turn, dear," said Hetty. A strand of hair had escaped from her tight little bun, giving her a wild look that really wasn't like her at all.

"Oh. Well. Um." He frowned at his plate for a moment and then said, "I was wondering if anyone has any experience of dealing with fussy eaters? Children, I mean. Jase Harris is in a terrible state because his eldest won't eat anything but peas all of a sudden."

There was a mutual murmur around the group, and interest passed on effortlessly from Cara and Mike's books to Jase Harris. Everyone had an opinion about parenting, it seemed.

But Berta had the distinct feeling she hadn't heard the last of Mike's books just yet.

Sure enough, when Berta returned home that evening, shaking rain off her wax-protected overcoat, the problem popped up again. On her kitchen table. A thick tome of a book, with a note that said, 'read these, love Mike' on the top.

An hour later Andrea arrived with Cara. They'd been to the village hall to finish making curtains for Cara's room. Cara had printed them herself. Not to Berta's taste, but it was clear the girl liked them, and that was all Berta needed to know. Cara looked tired, though. Berta gave her a plate of sliced fruits and nuts that she really liked, a slice of bread and jam and a mug of tea, and wasn't surprised when Cara decided to take them to her room.

Meanwhile, Andrea had taken the book to a chair beside the fire, and dived in with all the eagerness of the unjaded bibliophile that she was.

Berta put Andrea's tea and sandwich on the table by her chair, and went to poke the fire.

"This is horrible," Andrea said. "I can't believe they used to do this to people."

Berta straightened up, and braced herself. "Go on,

then."

"They tortured people who were unwell," Andrea said, in a small, wavery voice, very different to her usual measured tones.

"So I heard."

"You knew about this?"

"It's not a secret. I read my fair share of history books at University, you know."

"Oh. Oh, of course."

"I daresay your reading list was more about credit exchange systems than wellbeing practices." Andrea was an accountant, primarily. The Knowing had come late to her. It wasn't her fault.

"These books." Andrea took her hands from the volume, deserting it in her lap as if it was something dirty. "They're not what I expected."

Berta raised an eyebrow.

Andrea continued, "They're records. Kept by doctors. About the people they cared for. They called them 'patients'."

"I presume they'd have to be. Some of them waited a very long time to get better. Some of them never did."

"They locked them up," said Andrea. "Took them out of the world."

"That's what people tend to do with things they don't understand." Berta took her seat, opposite Andrea's, and noted the tears in her eyes, the anguish rolling off her in waves. "We don't do things that way any more. That's all that matters."

"They matter," said Andrea. "These people - Patient thirty-one, and forty-two, and the one that's simply called 'Miss X' for some reason. They were shunned by their community. Ignored, restrained, ridiculed. By strangers. They weren't treated." She dropped the book on the floor with a loud 'thud'. "They were silenced."

Berta let Andrea live her anger for a moment, and then she said, "What did you think of your first 'share, don't despair' meeting, then?"

A little smile appeared on Andrea's face. "At least the cake was nice."

"Acceptable," said Berta. "More tea?"

The next morning, Berta took a stroll through the Wellbeing Centre from the Crescent, through the Cafe where the thermal petals fluttered and turned to find the sun, and into the Social Space. It was one of her favourite places in White Water: there was a garden in the centre where a handful of people were planting out tender spring crops amid the primroses and aconites. People sat on comfortable sofas chatting or tapping away on devices. Blossom and Hetty were with Jase and his family in the kitchen area, making pizza for lunch. (Without peas, it appeared.)

And at the back of the social space was a big wall, which had, until a few weeks ago, been white. Now it was a bustling work in progress, images and stories bursting out of the blank brick canvas. Cara knelt on the floor, all her attention on the white crests of the river she was painting.

"Good morning," Berta said.

Cara looked up and smiled. She had a spot of blue paint on her nose, and a healthy flush to her cheeks. "Would you like to paint?" she asked in her soft, gentle voice.

"Not today, thank you." Berta spotted something in the painting, right down at the bottom, near the floor. There was a rock, one of the boulders that bordered the river in places. But under it were four letters, written in a crimson so dark you'd only see it up close. FEAR. "Cara, is that yours?"

Cara stared at it for a long while before she

nodded. She looked up at Berta and something unfurled like blossom blooming on an apple tree.

Berta's hand hovered over Cara's bare arm. "May I?"

Cara took Berta's hand and placed it on her skin.

The river tumbled through her mind, spinning its golden thread; the great dragon Sulis turned and churned through the water and opened her jaws in a scream so dark, so loud as to deafen the world; then twisted away in a stream of gold and silver, and Berta Knew.

She took Cara into her arms, tears rolling down her cheeks, and whispered, "I'm so sorry, child. So sorry."

Cara held on tight and said, "Thank you."

The next day Berta came into the kitchen in her dressing gown, as was her habit, to lay the table for breakfast and water the plants on the patio that needed it. She noticed Cara's sketch book open on the table. Berta glanced at it. The pages were decorated with ink drawings which surrounded lines of carefully written text.

I thought if I told you
It might all blow away
Like desert dust
A mirage?

I thought my pain would hurt you
Or you would think less
Or you would hate me
Beat me
Turn me out
To burn up in the fire of the sun.

But no

You gave me
Trust
And peace
In the cool blue-white
Of your river.

Cara

About the Contributors

ALEX WESTON teaches creative writing for Converge and has a MA in creative writing from York St John University. Under the pen name *Alys West* she writes contemporary fantasy and steampunk. Her novels *Beltane* and *The Dirigible King's Daughter* are published by Fabrian Books. She's currently working on her third novel, *Storm Witch* which will be published in summer 2019.

AMY STEWART is a York-based writer originally from Edinburgh. She can't resist darkly magical settings, or landscapes which become characters in themselves. A freelance Copywriter by day, she has a degree in English Language and Literature from Newcastle University and is currently studying for an MA in Creative Writing at York St John. Amy has a passion for performing her work – she was recently part of the *Enemies Project Camarade* Event and was chosen to speak at the launch for the *Beyond the Walls* anthology, in which she also features. Amy is a huge lover of circus arts, and when she's not writing, you'll probably find her trying out new tricks on the aerial silks.

CAROLINE lives in Yorkshire, her adopted home. This is her first foray into having her writing published. Maybe the first of many as there are a myriad of ideas and themes still to explore. Caroline is a dabbler, writing, reading and crafting is among the variety of activities she enjoys.

CATHERINE is a graduate in European studies with French. She has an interest in art, music and creative writing and has completed courses in these subjects at Converge. Likes tea and cake.

CF is trapped in the North of England. CF has no digital footprint. If you try to contact her she will not reply.

CHRISTINA O'REILLY loves lives in the North of England with her husband and cat. Other interests include walking, cooking, art, painting and pottery. As a new writer Christina is enjoying experimenting with different genres.

ELIZABETH McLOUGHLIN is a York based writer, originally from Scotland. The Mystery of the Chapel is her debut story. Elizabeth uses poetry as a way to escape and in inspired by read life situations. She enjoys song-writing, guitar and cross stitch and is a people person.

EMMA McKENZIE loves playing with words and often records short sketches of family life and events that have struck a chord with her. She is interested in autobiographical writing and leads the Converge Memoir and Autobiographical writing course as well as a Connect to Nature creative writing class at St Nicks nature reserve. Emma loves connecting with people through story sharing and story making.

ESTHER CLARE began writing stories about her favourite toy monkey when she was five. Since then she has written short stories, poetry, memoirs and a novel. She writes about a quirky childhood in Northern Ireland - close friends, tin baths, wine gums, and the puzzled intrigue of bomb scares. Esther has an MA in English from Edinburgh University. In the last few years an Eco-Therapy project inspired her to write about nature and life. St Nicks Nature Reserve have published a collection of her poetry on their website. She recently completed a Converge Memoir and Autobiography course and is keen to develop her writing further. Esther is also a songwriter turning poetry into music.

HELEN KENWRIGHT writes speculative and queer fiction, and teaches creative writing. She is Creative Writing Lead for Converge. Her publications include 'Women of White Water' in *Glass and Gardens: Solarpunk Summers*, 'Seeds of White Water' in *Terra Two: An Ark for Off-World Survival*, 'Smoke' in *Forest* and 'Drop in the Ocean' in *Ocean*. Her winning entry in the @SFFiction competition is published in *Serious Flash Fiction 4*.

She lives in York with two cats, and plays more video games than is seemly for a woman of her age.

HOLLY lives near York. She has dabbled in poetry and prose for over a decade. In her free time, you will find her drafting ideas for a future novel, surrounded by a growing number of unread books, hunting for inspiration. Holly is unable to form a coherent sentence without music, tea, and a spellchecker. Holly is a published author having also written for the first anthology.

IAIN BARCLAY was first published in 1998 in 'Fifty Routes through Mongolia'. It would be twenty years until he was published again in the first edition of 'Creative Writing Heals' which included his short story 'Awen's Needle'. He is currently working towards enrolling on a degree in creative writing at York St John University. Iain's writing tends to reflect his tenuous grip on reality and a healthy disrespect for our illustrious leaders in society.

IAN JARVIS was born and lives in York. He first became interested in Doctor Who when he was three years old, and in Egyptian history and mythology when he was five. He wrote his first short story, about Hercules and Hydra, at Fulford Cross School. He would like to write a series of novels about a different Time Lord, with many planets, time periods, friends and foe, old and new, for everyone to enjoy.

JOANNE has always loved reading and has discovered through Converge an even greater love of writing. She has a particular leaning towards the dark and the absurd and is enjoying experimenting with different genres and themes.

Her only regret is that there are far too many wonderful things to read and write about, so many ideas to explore that she wishes she'd started far earlier!

JULIE did not come from a family of writers, but she knew she wanted to write from a very early age. She finds words fascinating, especially how just a few well-chosen words can evoke the strongest of emotions. She has taken up short story writing only recently but has found the succinctness needed for it to be refreshing.

JUNIOR CRYLE was born and raised in the City of York, and lives with creativity as a self-certified dragon fanatic, from a love of illustrations to an interest in mythology. An optimist when it comes to fiction and life, he reflects this trait in his work as he takes pride in giving enjoyment to those around him. A silver tongue in conversation and a black belt in Karate, he is a force to be reckoned with.

KEITH is from North Yorkshire. He has done creative writing for a number of years. Some of it has been put into books for people to enjoy. He tries to rhyme his poetry but it's not always possible. He is classed as a mature student. He feels the help from Alex and Helen have given him has given him confidence to express his writing and do more poetry which he enjoys. He's also done a film and art course with Converge.

KEVIN PAYLOR is a published Poet and has also published articles in magazines on nautical and social/community issues. He is a former Merchant Navy Officer, Prison Officer, and Community Development Manager. He also worked in Catering, Landscape Gardening, Factory Production and Machine Operator, Assistant Manager of a Bookmakers and as a Social Worker. Kevin is a campaigner/activist for many concerns including, welfare of ex sea-forces and housing issues. Formerly Independent Anarchist candidate for Clifton.
Kevin's interests and hobbies include antique furniture renovation and collection, science, tinkering with old radios. All things pink and Crystal Palace F.C. Lives with his wife Christine and two dogs Sedale and Rosie.

LEANNE CAIRNS is 32 and lives in Chapelfields, York. She lives with her Mum and her brother. Creative writing has opened Leanne's world immensely as she uses a wheelchair and it's hard for her to get around. Converge and creative writing has made her meet lots of amazing new people.

LYNNE PARKIN is a true Yorkshire Parkin. A fifty something female who lives with her husband, a Bedlington terrier and a black cat. She is also a much loved grandma and behind her smile you will find a paperback serial killer who loves short stories, poetry and play writing.

LYKAELL DERT-ETHRAE was born in the suburbs of Aldvon on Covyn 5. She is currently one of the most prolific publishers on Ancient History for the Covyn Historical Society (CHS) and holds one of the chairs on their Board. Her best friend is renowned Project C, the only person in Covyn to publish more books on

Ancient History than Lykaell. She currently resides in Lios where the headquarters of the CHS sits. Lykaell spends her free time running around like a little girl hugging trees and chasing cats as well as going off to exotic archaeological expeditions with her friend Project C.

MICHAEL lives somewhere around York. He did at one point have chickens as pets and still treats their disappearance as suspicious. He enjoys painting, drawing and sculpting when he can get peace and quiet.

PATRICK LAWN lives in York. He does various other Converge courses including theatre and Discovering Museums. He's a member of Communitas Choir and volunteers at York Explore library. His hobbies include swimming and going to see York City play.

ROSS is new author who lives in England. He enjoys reading, gaming and writing, of course.

RUTH is Yorkshire born and returned to the county she loves in 2005 after time spent in London and the Midlands. An avid reader, Ruth has worked with the Ilkley Literature Festival as Fringe coordinator. She has also facilitated writing for well-being sessions with homeless people, people with head injuries, young people, including those in care. She is a trustee of, and volunteer with several health, arts, and LGBT organisations, nationally and locally. With a lifelong passion for tennis, Ruth is now finding herself to be quite a competitive but not a very competent boccia player!

SANDRA lives in York with her seven gerbils. She enjoys shopping, going to the cinema and babysitting her sister's four children. *The Test of Life* is her debut piece.

SOPHIE is 19 and lives in North Yorkshire. She's a Psychology student and volunteers with Converge in her spare time. When she's not studying, you can find her riding horses, at the gym, or spending time with her friends.

SUE RICHARDSON lives in York with her husband and dog, Stan. Sue writes crime fiction and is fascinated by seemingly everyday characters who have a dark moral compass underneath. Hopefully she will show you everyone has a breaking point. *The Send-Off* is her debut piece.

TIM lives in York and enjoys creative writing and sport. Needs different life experiences to added to his creative writing. This year enjoy the zip wires of Dalby Forest, and somehow survived otherwise none of the above. The idea for Tim's piece came from how we used to have a great city with family run businesses but they are now being neutralised. I hope by reading this the reader will get involved with speaking out about the city and help to make York a good place not just to live now but in the future,

WILLIAM writes short fiction mostly set in York, where he lives. He loves reading, especially the short stories of Lorrie Moore, Ali Smith and Sarah Hall.

About Converge

Converge is a partnership between York St John University and mental health service providers in the York region. It offers high quality educational opportunities to those who use NHS and non-statutory mental health services and who are 18 years and over.

Converge was established in 2008 from a simple idea: to offer good quality courses in a university setting to local people who use mental health services taught by students and staff. The development of Converge has progressively demonstrated the potential of offering educational opportunities to people who use mental health services, delivered by students and staff and held on a university campus. This has become the key principle which, today, remains at the heart of Converge. Born of a unique collaboration between the NHS and York St John University, Converge continues to deliver educational opportunities for people with mental health problems.

We offer work-based experience to university students involved in the programme. All classes are taught by undergraduate and postgraduate students, staff and, increasingly people who have lived experience of mental ill health. We have developed a solid track record of delivering quality courses. Careful support and mentoring underpin our work, thereby allowing students to experiment with their own ideas and creativity whilst gaining real world experience in the community. This undoubtedly enhances their employability in an increasingly competitive market.

As a leader in the field, Converge develops symbiotic projects and partnerships which are driven by innovation and best practice. The result is twofold:

a rich and exciting educational opportunity for people with mental health problems alongside authentic and practical work experience for university students.

The aims of Converge are to:

- Work together as artists and students
- Build a community where we learn from each other
- Engage and enhance the university and wider community
- Provide a supportive and inclusive environment
- Respect others and value ourselves
- Above all, strive to be ordinary, extraordinary yet ourselves

About the Writing Tree

The Writing Tree is dedicated to the support and nurturing of creative writers. Founded in 2011, the Writing Tree offers one-to-one tuition, coaching and editing services and range of online and community courses.

The guiding principles of the Writing Tree are that creative writing has importance independent of subject, purpose or audience, and that everyone has the right to write, and to write what they wish.

The Writing Tree is honoured to publish 'Creative Writing Heals' for Converge. All proceeds from the book are donated to further the efforts of Converge writers.

You can find out more about the Writing Tree at www.writingtree.co.uk.

Acknowledgements

Thank you to all our contributors, for having the courage to share their fantastic work.

Thank you to Laurie Farnell for his lovely cover art.

Thank you to Susi Liarte of the Writing Tree for graphic design.

Thank you to all the Converge students, mentors, supporters and YSJ students for their help.

Thank you to Nick and Emma for their vision, advice, support and passion – and for having faith in us.

Thank you to all the staff at Converge for all they've done to support this production.

Thank you to our friends at Mind and York Explore.

Thank you to the Igen Trust for resourcing and encouraging us.

And finally, thanks to our production team of Alex, Helen, Andy, Amy, Clare and William for being a magnificent crew for the 2019 voyage of the Great Ship Overly Ambitious!

40746759R00120

Printed in Poland
by Amazon Fulfillment
Poland Sp. z o.o., Wrocław